LOVE IS PARTICIPATION IN ETERNITY

LOVE IS PARTICIPATION IN ETERNITY

Udayan Vajpeyi

Translated from Hindi by Poonam Saxena

BLOOMSBURY
NEW DELHI • LONDON • OXFORD • NEW YORK • SYDNEY

BLOOMSBURY INDIA
Bloomsbury Publishing India Pvt. Ltd
Second Floor, LSC Building No. 4, DDA Complex, Pocket C – 6 & 7,
Vasant Kunj, New Delhi, 110070

BLOOMSBURY, BLOOMSBURY INDIA and the Diana logo
are trademarks of Bloomsbury Publishing Plc

Originally published in Hindi as *Qayas* by Rajkamal Prakashan, 2019
First published in English in India 2025

ISBN: PB: 978-93-61317-93-4
eBook: 978-93-61312-70-0

2 4 6 8 10 9 7 5 3 1

Typeset in Fournier MT Manipal Technologies Limited
Printed and bound in India by Thomson Press India Ltd

For sale in the Indian subcontinent only

MIX
Paper | Supporting responsible forestry
FSC® C010615

To find out more about our authors and books visit www.bloomsbury.com and sign up for our newsletters

For Alpana

I like sitting and reading in different libraries. That is why I visit many big cities all year long. But I always spend the winters in my ancestral city. The library there is very dear to me. This winter, it was shut for an entire week. As a matter of fact, it is the library that draws me to my native place. I would climb the stairs to the library every morning and stand at the huge door. The time to open the doors would pass but nobody would turn up. In the pale sunlight that fell on the stairs, I'd stare at the big nails hammered into the copper-plated old door and then leave, walking down the stairs. Outside in the green maidan were a few squat, dense trees. Thin mist, like wisps of light-blue wool, enveloped the trees from all sides. Swirling above the grass, it seemed to prevent the sunshine from spilling down, as if to soak up the light before it could reach the grass. Some mornings, the mist would be so thick, it seemed like the sky had slid down, its strands reaching out to touch every blade of grass. I would go away, leaving behind my dejection at not being able to enter the library with the lost grass searching for the sun. One morning, while going home, I heard at the chai thela that a special person connected to the library had died. No matter how important he may have been, does a public place like a library shut down for so many days just because a person has died? A day later, I heard that this special person was the one who had started this library; it had been closed for decades before he arrived. Generations of termites had gnawed their way through the books caged inside broken almirahs. When he came here, he worked night and day on the old building that housed the closed library, restored every single book, catalogued each one, and had the musty floor washed with neem water every day for three or four months to rid it of the termites and other germs that had settled there, so that one could sit down on it. In the beginning, he would read alone in the library. Once in a way, someone would drop in to read. It took time, but slowly people started coming.

The strange thing is that I've been coming to the library for a few days every winter for the last five years, but I've never even seen this gentleman. Perhaps this is a measure of the library's smooth functioning: the person who ran it remained invisible. Now that he is gone, will the library be deserted once again? When it reopened after a full week, I went in and saw that everything, from the floor to the walls and the ceiling, was spotless, and like before, people were sitting in the chairs placed around the long tables, reading books and newspapers. I didn't feel even for a moment that someone who belonged here had departed for another world. But who was this man who hadn't gone though he was gone? Who hadn't died though he was dead?

People are entering the gate, some in cars, some on scooters, some on foot. Everyone's faces are alight with a quiet excitement. The long rays of the setting sun unfurl deep shadows of the people getting off cars and scooters. Those on foot bring their own long shadows with them.

Kishore

Now he will live like a ghost in the library. He will wander between the book racks. He will thicken on the floor like layers of dust. He will lie on the grimy skylights like sunlight. He will stick to the old curtains like dirt. Why be sad? Whatever happened was fine. I will never step inside that place as long as I live. What if the wretch, even now, clings to my feet like dust? Those stairs, those corridors, that balcony ... How can I pluck them out of my mind, how can I wipe those books away from my memories! Anyway, now bats will make their home among those books.

Whatever happened was fine. Absolutely fine. It wasn't possible for anything else to have happened. Not in the slightest. It's not that I'm particularly delighted at everything that happened – no, no, I'm not. Even if I wanted to, I couldn't say that I am happy with everything that transpired. I really want to be happy about everything that happened. To laugh and keep laughing. To go in every direction, to cover each direction, every tiny particle, with my laughter. I want to hug everyone I meet. To start laughing suddenly and very loudly. To see my ringing laughter scatter everywhere, wherever I look. To catch sight of my smiling face in the mirror of my own laughter. Of course, I want this. But I can't. Despite so desperately wanting to be happy, I am not happy. Yes, I am not sad – of that I am certain. No, I am not sad. Let me say it again and again: I am not sad. Nor is there a shadow of regret about me. Not even as small as the shadow cast by a flying bird on the green grass.

This is the only end he could have had. Exactly this. Yes, yes, this is exactly what should have happened. What else could have happened to him? What else happens to people like this? He got what he should have got, how was that wrong? This was what was written for him. The writing has been written from before, and you simply have to surrender yourself to it, silently, without a word. He too submerged himself in it. He slipped and went on slipping. No matter how scary it appears from the outside, it seems so right, so appropriate from the inside.

No matter what anyone says to me, I'm not sad that Vandana also slipped. Even though she did not slip outside of her life, even though her face reflects her disdain, anger and pity towards me – why just me, towards all of us – even though her voice may have turned lifeless in her eyes, I am not sad that she has become like this. She trod a path that could have had no other outcome. All by herself, absolutely by herself, despite me, despite all of us, she trod such a path that she had to slip outside of herself. Why just me, no one will feel bad about it.

Everyone has to suffer, *Vando rani*, *badi siyani*, very clever; so what if you are my niece, did you think that would save you? Is there anyone who hasn't suffered? Has anyone ever escaped the wrath of the universe's power that you would escape it?

Was there anyone whose eyes did not reflect the shamelessness of what she was doing. So much shamelessness in what she kept doing, quietly. How she put my pride – our pride – on the line. The same pride that I, actually all of us, accumulated, bit by bit. What about that? The difficulties we endured to make a place for ourselves in this city. So much hard work. Is there no value to my, rather our, hard work? I stood for hours in trains when I travelled to Kashmir, returning with saffron, and the entire household spent day after day packing it into small boxes. Only then was it ready for sale. This was a waste for Vandana, all of this. How did she even think she could do what she did with such shamelessness. Oh God, a simple home like ours, and she, she did everything. Did she never think of us, not even once? Did our ancestors, hanging on the walls of our house for years, with their large moustaches and beards, never cross her mind even once? Did she never think, not even once, what would happen to me, to us, to those ancestors, when she did all that she did? Where would we hide, how would we show ourselves to the people of this town?

Did she have no responsibility towards us? Not even a little bit? Does it fall only to our lot to be responsible? Doesn't she get to share the responsibility even a bit? No, no, whatever happened to her should have happened. This is how it was ordained by destiny, this is how it should have been ordained by destiny. I'm not at all sad about it. The people of the town are with me, my ancestors are with me, the sun and the stars are with me. Look, no one is mourning that she faltered, no one is shedding any tears over the way she has turned silent, mute. In the end, everything broke the way it had to break.

Oh! My left eye, this stupid eye, why is it blinking convulsively, what am I babbling on about, and why, why?

Soft whispers fly about in every corner of the hall. The back door opens a crack, less than halfway through, and a manlike shape seems to slip through that opening and come inside. On the stage, an empty chair slowly rocks back and forth like a shadow.

Vandana

Look, that voice is lost. It has returned to the rustling of leaves, the patter of feet, the sound of children crying, women sobbing. It has gone back to where it most likely came from. I remained safe, untouched, but the voice vanished. I know now it won't be possible to retrieve it from the rustling of leaves, the patter of feet, the crying of children, the wailing women. Even if I could somehow wrench back every single fibre of that voice from all these places, in whose throat would I weave them together? Without the warp and weft of a fabric, how would I stitch together the fine, soft cloth of that voice which, every time I heard it, would unfurl like a gossamer-thin sheet, like harsingar flowers. But then, why do I keep thinking that if I want to, I can do this. Why do I keep thinking that if I try, I can still accomplish, with my own hands, that which is not possible at all. Perhaps it is this very wish that has trapped me within myself, like a yellowing leaf on the branch of this shrivelled body. This same desire traps every broken person, like a yellowing leaf on the branch of her shrivelled body, for a moment or two, for year on year. Who knows? But I know this desire is merely an illusion of life, only meant to keep my body surviving till the end. How cruelly it is intent on saving itself, by making use of me. How shamelessly this life is coursing through my veins, trembling in my muscles, bubbling over in my dreams. As if it has placed a begging bowl before me, beseeching me to save it.

It was Sudipt who had told me in his extremely soft voice, when we used to sit on the stairs by the pond every day, at least those days we met every day, staring at the sun's rays flickering in the green water. It was he who had told me, in that same voice which seemed to come from the far end of a cavernous cave, that no one knew when his mother disappeared within herself while searching for a sound, any sound, from her deceased husband. 'No, no,' he had said, 'she hadn't died, she just got lost somewhere within herself and everybody felt that she had died.' Perhaps this is what people mean when they use the word 'dying'. Disappearing to some place within yourself from where you can't come back. To get rid of them, two children were left alone and defenceless in a forest, so that wild animals would devour them, but the children were clever and, moreover, determined to stay alive, so they kept dropping white stones on the ground while entering the jungle, and once they were left alone, they followed the trail of stones to return home. From the jaws of death, they came back into the embrace of life. Similarly, we keep dropping white stones as we progressively get lost within ourselves and we keep coming back. How cleverly we make a pretence, time and again, of getting lost, and again and again, without any effort, we suddenly come back. But there are a few people, very few, a couple of them, like his mother, who disappear within themselves without the white stones and don't come back. The remaining people who are used to the idea of coming back, who find it natural to come back, they smile slightly and, with a tinge of sorrow and profound self-satisfaction, point out how that poor soul could not come back. They think that this person forgot to take with him the articles necessary for his return when he journeyed within himself. But those who are caught in the never-ending trap of saving themselves at any cost never find out, as they go inside themselves, that it is life that is repeatedly handing them the white stones so that they can return and life can once again succeed in saving itself. But then, it's as if they leave those stones, those unfulfilled desires, those pulsating expressions of the past – all the things they need to come back – in the corner of their table and then go away inside themselves. That's how his mother left the white stones on her table, and searching for a sound, any sound from his father, got lost within herself.

But I? What should I do? I, who see his smile at every road that leads me within myself. Not just his smile, I see all of him standing there, and each time, I fail to get lost in the forest within me, and this life of mine, this long, miserable life, this cruel life, quietly extends its span inside me. The remainder of this meaningless life is filled with a quivering fear of and agitation over what might happen, and Kishore chacha thinks, Ma does too, that I am not in my senses, that I am adrift. How will anyone know that this girl, sitting in a corner, head resting on her knees, can't find the way to disappear inside herself. It is no one's fault. They don't even know that life unconsciously sticks to people like a leech and then, in so many ways, hollows them out. How will they know that floundering about, I run from one door to another, and at each door a faint sound indicating his presence makes me pause. Each time I think I am deluding myself, but I sense this only when the illusion has worked on me. I step back from the door and go in search of the next one. This is the power of the illusion, while it's there, it doesn't seem like an illusion. Only when it is gone does it reveal its truth. Is this reality also an illusion that hasn't yet passed? I believe it is an illusion, and I step back. But before the illusion can pass, before it is over, I start running towards the next door.

How can I describe that right now, at this very moment, I can see him standing before me, wearing the same striped shirt, the same blue trousers, the same shoes – I am certain this isn't Sudipt, it is not even his shadow, just a cruel attempt on the part of life to save itself inside my body, but how can I convince myself it isn't him. It is him!

In the faded yellow light, a thread of sound is audible. 'I've heard a lot about this show.'

Sneha

I had told Vandana earlier too. But she had laughingly avoided the subject. As if I was talking about something impossible. 'My uncle and brother would never do anything of the sort, after all, they've been his friends,' she would say. After I repeatedly told her that her uncle and brother would do it precisely because he'd been their friend, and they constantly felt he was deceiving them, she said, 'No, Sneha, they're incapable of it. They won't attack him, not because they've been his friends – this much I know – but because they don't have the gall. They're scared.'

She had faith, Vandana did, even if it was just a bit, that her uncle and brother were cowards; she was so sure they didn't have the guts to do anything, that they weren't bold enough. She failed to see that, to keep itself safe, cowardice often transforms into fearlessness. It can accomplish quite a lot. And then go back to crouching in its shell. She failed to see that no human emotion is ever pure. I have always felt emotions can't be pure or unadulterated, perhaps because I have always kept my distance from every emotion. I never thought of cowardice as a pure emotion; I always saw it mixed with fearlessness and wonder. I have seen a glimmer of affection even in an emotion like contempt, felt a layer of attraction floating like mist above the surface of feelings of disgust and loathing.

I had told Vandana many times, but she was completely convinced of their cowardice, perhaps because she saw every emotion the way she saw her own love: pure, made only of itself. Who knows, it may even be true. Perhaps love is the only emotion that is wholly pure – but not because it doesn't contain any other feelings within itself. It does. In fact, it carries more feelings compared to other emotions, but all of them, once they arrive at love, lose their own colour and take on the colour of love. Anger is no longer anger, it becomes a part of love; fear is no longer fear but becomes a part of love. Is that why Vandana, sunk deep in love, couldn't see the recklessness in cowardice, standing silently in a corner holding a knife? I am saying she didn't see it, but the truth is she made no effort to see it. She thought this was fair. Whenever I went to see Vandana, I saw more than one knife on their bodies, below their staring eyes. Ready to attack. But covered by a thin film of civility.

All she thought of every day was how she was going to meet him the next evening, where she was going to meet him the next evening. She hadn't forgotten the time and place, had she? She never imagined that someday someone else could plan to meet him in the night in between the two evenings. Quietly, without her knowing. Even after so many days, no one has been able to find out who, in the darkness of the night, had counted his last few breaths, those breaths in whose rise and fall Vandana had seen her own limitlessness.

The entire city was preoccupied with fanciful investigations into the causes of his death. Many had told me about their theories. Perhaps because I was Vandana's friend. But was being a friend akin to being a trash can where anyone could dump whatever garbage they wanted? Not that the storytellers cared. Everyone described Sudipt's death as if they'd been there at the scene. As if the whole city was standing around him when he was dying. Some people suspected her uncle and brother, but no one could say for sure. In such cases, though, it is only suspicion that can throw some light on the matter. Other people said it was his wife's doing, but here too, no one could say so with certainty. I had sensed that she was also deeply attached to Sudipt. All you could see in her eyes was love for Sudipt. Her attachment to Sudipt may have been different from Vandana's, but it wasn't less by any means. It was born out of a deep sense of caring for Sudipt. A few people believed Vandana's uncle and brother did this in collusion with his wife. She was the one who'd opened the door for them late at night, and they tiptoed inside and did what they had wanted to do for so many days. But nobody is fully convinced of any of these stories. This is also because everyone knows that her uncle and brother were not in the city that night – they had gone to Jammu to buy provisions for their shop. And his wife had spent the night in the hospital since she was ill. But people also wonder why they went to Jammu the very night his wife was admitted to the hospital. Or why Mridula was admitted to the hospital the same night the two of them were out of town.

When I hear one of these stories, I start believing it too, but when the next one comes along, that belief melts in the heat of the new story. I keep running from one story to the other, unable to stick to any. Sometimes I see her uncle and brother holding a knife, sometimes I see Mridula, then I see the knives falling from their hands again and again. Sometimes I find the idea of them holding a knife strange and sometimes I find the idea of each of them holding a bloody knife absolutely natural. My suspicion is like a pawn on a chessboard – sometimes I pick it up and place it in one square, sometimes in another, and sometimes I find it stuck in my hand with no vacant square left to put it. Then I scream and toss this good–bad suspicion in the air like a stone and feel lighter. It is true that Mridula, steeped in envy, could have done this, but it is also true that she could only have done this if she'd been so blinded by envy that no other solution was visible to her. But didn't she know of Sudipt's deep love for her? Self-loving people like Vandana's brother and uncle wouldn't have put their own lives in danger just because of their sister or niece. Do people who are so self-absorbed put themselves in this kind of danger under any circumstances? But if not them, then who could have murdered Sudipt? If you look at it one way, any of them could have done it, but if you look at it from another angle, then none of them would be guilty.

Death is anyway wrapped in an enigma. And then sometimes, it gives this secrecy a kind of shape which constantly pokes you. Wrapped in pain, we keep returning to this enigma and retreat every time after suffering a strange kind of hurt. Many times, I think that whatever had to happen has happened. Sudipt is gone, now we must think of Vandana, we must pay attention to her condition. But I know that Vandana is deeply stricken by the way Sudipt went, she would have been beside herself no matter how he went, but then she could have brought God between Sudipt and herself, that it was God's doing; now, however, given the way he went, all she can see is an unknown shadow standing between Sudipt and his death. 'Sneha, how could anyone do this?' This mystery is like a thorn deeply embedded in her separation from him and every now and then it throbs with pain: 'How could anyone do this?'

Children are not allowed. But they're not sent back either. They play in the grass, in the yard outside the hall. There is sand at the foot of the slide. The children chase one another as they move in a circle on the small merry-go-round. The gardener sits in a corner of the yard, smiling at them. He takes the beedi hidden in the hollow of his left hand to his lips, trying to make the smoke dissolve into the evening twilight as soon as it escapes his mouth.

Noa

Everyone stopped playing long ago. Piddu's ball had gone into the bushes; we kept searching for it but didn't find it. Sonali said, 'We'll search tomorrow, we can't look for it in the dark now.' The children agreed instantly. All of them left for their homes. I kept sitting at the edge of the empty maidan. I was a little anxious that he would come to know I had reached home late. It wasn't my fault that I was late returning from the maidan. Lakhna came late to pick me up. He must've been sitting, smoking a beedi at the paan shop on the way. When Bakul's sister came to pick her up, she had asked if I wanted to leave with them. I don't know why I refused and kept sitting on the steps at the edge of the maidan, waiting for Lakhna. It started getting dark. The trees around me turned into smudges. I heard the bells of the nearby temple so clearly, it was as if they were ringing right next to me. Everything that appears far away in the daylight seems so near in the dark, as if it has crept close to you. The sound of the crickets too became much louder. He came very late. On the way back, I kept asking him questions as I do every day, and he kept mumbling something about memsaab, memsaab. Amma was not at home. Her fever had shot up and she had gone to the hospital; she would probably stay the night there. If her fever came down, she would be back in the morning. With some difficulty, Lakhna told me that he had taken her to the hospital and that was why he was late coming to the maidan. Even though it wasn't my fault, I was a little scared. I kept hoping Baba wouldn't find out I had come back late. Otherwise, as soon as he returned from the library, he would get angry: 'Why didn't you come back with Bakul's sister? If Lakhanlal hadn't come the whole night, would you have sat in the maidan all night waiting for him? Couldn't Bakul have stayed with you a little longer? How could Bakul's sister, that foolish girl, leave you alone there?' I knew that once he discovered I had come late, he would be as anxious as he would have been had I still not been back. Anxious and troubled, he'd pace the room and call Lakhna again and again, question him again and again about my coming late. He would ask so many times that even I would start believing I wasn't home but still sitting alone in the maidan waiting for Lakhna who was never going to turn up.

He will interrogate me so often, I will feel as if I have fallen asleep on the steps at the maidan's edge. That's when the wide, sprawling stairs will shrink and become narrow. Without thinking, I start walking down the stairs. There is darkness everywhere, the silence only broken by the chirping of crickets, and I keep going down the ever-extending stairs. On the way I find Lakhna lying on the stairs and when he sees me coming towards him, he gets up hastily, dusts his dhoti and begins descending the stairs ahead of me till he vanishes. I will try and call out to him urgently, but my voice will flounder in my throat and falter. Now I will be left standing midway on those dark stairs, and from behind me I'll hear baba's voice: 'Noa, why haven't you come home yet?' I will try to turn back to go to him, but my feet will be stuck on the stairs. He'll ask me so many times that I will think I still haven't returned and feel the anxiety building up. Trapped in these thoughts, I will start feeling very scared. I can't say this to Baba. Or to anyone else. This is his way of showing his fear and worry. The person he worries about also feels scared for herself for no reason whatsoever. This was baba's way. I don't know if he even knew this.

Lakhna, sleeping on the carpet nearby, began snoring. The lane outside the window was empty and desolate. Somewhere a dog cried out. Off and on, the lights from speeding cars would shine on the window and then fade away. Baba hadn't come yet. I tried to wake up Lakhna a few times, but he just mumbled, half asleep, 'Bibi ji, he'll be here soon,' and began snoring again.

Amma is alone in the hospital, I am alone here, and Baba is stuck who knows where. Maybe he got to know that amma is in the hospital and went straight there. But he would definitely have phoned. He would have called as soon as he reached the hospital. Which means he doesn't know. I don't have the number of his phone in the library. Lakhna will know, but he's refusing to get up. 'Lakhna, Lakhna, get up, wake up, look, Baba still hasn't come, call him ... Lakhna, Lakhna, Lakhanlal, Lakhanlal.' I kept trying to wake him up. But he remained sprawled on the carpet. Defeated, I lay down on the bed and drew the blanket up to my face. Sleep was a little distance away, gently stroking my eyes. But it didn't come to me. The phone rang. I threw off the blanket and ran. It was Baba. 'Noa, you haven't slept yet, you can't sleep? Give Mridula the phone.' 'She's gone to the hospital,' I replied. 'Why, what happened?' 'She had high fever; she might stay there tonight.' His voice started shaking. 'Are you alone? Where is Lakhna, why didn't he phone me?' 'He's here, sleeping. He's not getting up, I'm fed up, I'm scared. Come home quickly,' I said, almost in tears. 'There's nothing to be scared of, I'll come immediately.' He put down the phone.

As soon as I heard he'd be home soon, my fear began dissipating. It seems Lakhna had heard our conversation. He sat up on the carpet, wide awake, rubbing his eyes. He had probably heard me telling Baba that he'd been sleeping. Lakhna has this quality. He'll hear important things that concern him even in his sleep. He could do it then, he can do it now. He realised he could not avoid a scolding from Baba. Even before Baba comes home, I can hear his scolding booming in my ear: 'Why do you keep sleeping, were you pushing a mountain all day? You are impossible! You're becoming good for nothing!' When Lakhna is reduced to a complete state of panic, eyes darting here and there, then Baba will stop scolding him and say with a half-smile, his eyes dancing, 'Tell me, Lakhna, why do you make a stranger of yourself by saying "Lakhanlal" instead of "I" when you talk? Tell us, let Noa also hear why. Arre, tell us, don't feel shy!' And then Lakhna will say, as he always does, 'How can Lakhanlal have the temerity to refer to himself as "I", saheb? A poor man is a stranger to himself. If I don't call myself Lakhanlal, what should I say? What can I say ...'

Lakhna's voice echoed in my mind for a long time. As if he was saying the same thing hundreds of times. Thinking that Baba will be here soon, my eyelids grew heavy, and it seemed as if sleep, standing a little distance away, was coming towards me, slowly, softly. Its hands have the same feel as baba's hands. It lifts me with baba's hands and gently takes me into its lap. For the very last time, for when I woke up in the morning, the house was full of people. Baba was gone. He still hasn't come back.

As soon as she entered the gate, the girl raised her left hand to the back of her head and began stroking her hair. She smiled and then suddenly looked worried. She turned and ran towards the gate. Her dark blue scarf was lying next to it, swathed in sunlight and mist.

Mridula

The darkness of the night had entered, trembling, into my eyes. I could sense the pounding of each vein. If I stayed at home, the fever would shoot up, I wouldn't be able to manage, and Sudipt would have to bear the burden of my sickness. After some time I went to the hospital. All night I couldn't sleep, thinking that he should've come here, at least for a while. Lakhna could have looked after Noa. Doesn't Lakhna do that often anyway? He has never disregarded me like this before. Sometimes I felt he had created a narrow rift between us, but it was buried under so many layers of normal behaviour that, though it was present, it seemed as if it wasn't there. As if the thread of our relationship had broken at a point it was impossible to put a finger on. The sting from that rupture never went away. No, it wasn't neglect or disregard. He never did that, not even once. This was the first time. Had that hidden rift come out in the open? I kept tossing and turning in bed. I was thinking about myself, and he went away that night itself. I shouldn't have gone to the hospital. It was just a fever and, no matter how high, the temperature would have come down on its own. I'd been getting a fever for many nights now, but every night I'd felt the temperature come down. The same thing could have happened that night too. I could have stayed in bed at home and the fever would have broken late at night. It would have gone and perhaps Sudipt could have been saved. Even if the fever had stayed, I could have spent the night burning in its heat, and Sudipt wouldn't have gone away like he did. Why did I lose my patience, why didn't I stay calm? He had struggled so much to teach me how to stay calm and patient. But I failed at the moment when it mattered the most. It's not like I always listened to everything he said, but patience – that I learnt from him, slowly, after putting in much effort. I couldn't have lived with him without that. Though who knows whether I could have lived with him or not. Who knows whether I was living with him or not. We lived together, but I was alone. He too was alone, but that was the only way of living he knew. Yes, I was completely alone even while living with him. That was the only way I could be with him. Today, when he's not here, I am still alone. But there's a difference between these two ways of being alone: the aloneness I felt with him felt full – it was an aloneness brimming over with life, and I could peep in whenever I wanted; I could see, even touch, my sick father's face, the deep calmness of my invalid mother, my younger sister's airs and graces, the full expanse of Noa's childhood, the pages fluttering in Vandana's hands. His going emptied out my aloneness. Completely. Now I can only see my own face when I peep inside. With his going, it was as if the world within me disappeared like a mirage. My father is no longer there, lying on his deathbed; nor my mother losing the use of her limbs one after another; nor my sister sulking at every small thing; nor little Noa learning to walk by holding on to a table; nor I splashing about in a hilly waterfall; nor Vandana walking briskly down the side of the street. No, no, maybe they're still here, but lifeless, as if, with his passing, they have turned to wood.

Oh, where did that splinter go, which I carried with me all the years I spent with him. His tilting towards Vandana – that splinter! How I used to spend so many nights thinking of Vandana. How I would examine every fibre of her being as if under a microscope for hours on end, hoping I could turn him away from Vandana and towards myself. How long it took for the mystery to clear, that envy may be a crooked path, but it's a path that leads to your beloved nonetheless. I can no longer hide that it was through Vandana that I could feel Sudipt. This realisation came after so long. What I thought of as a splinter was in fact a way to reach him, though what a difficult way it was!

I'd constantly make accusations against him, constantly curse him, but as soon as he came before me, all my accusations seemed hollow, all my fears baseless. As soon as I saw him before me, I found my doubts trivial and unworthy, my envy squalid, as if it was polluting my mind. But as soon as I'd go away from him, the same thoughts would start clouding my mind again. I knew my fears were unfounded, my doubts without substance, even so, I was restless and uneasy that he would be snatched away from me, and I would be left alone. I would listen to everything he said very carefully, to make sure he wasn't being too clever by half. I kept track – as far as possible – of his every movement, to find out if it was a prelude to his leaving me. I even listened carefully to him mumbling in his sleep, thinking that maybe it would help me find a basis for my fear. I would go through the books he'd read, from the first page to the last, so that I might find something that would help me understand his actions. I found nothing, nothing I didn't already know.

I often secretly went to watch Vandana's shows. She used to choose passages from poems, plays, short stories, novels and essays from the ancient period, the Middle Ages and contemporary literature, which had some sort of affinity with each other, which, as she would say in her introduction, 'speak to each other without knowing each other'. She would translate into Hindi those parts which were not in Hindi, then link them together and read them out on the first Saturday of every month to a modest audience in a small hall. The spotlight would shine on her hands holding the pages, she herself would sit outside the circle of light on the small stage. All you could see were her fair hands shuffling the pages, and softly, her voice would fill the hall with images and thoughts from different cultures and eras. A Ghalib couplet would follow some sentence from the *Chandogya Upanishad*, from which would quietly glide out a line by Nirala, which would go on to merge into some esoteric observation by Marcel Proust.

I would watch the Show, enraptured. I would forget that I had not come to watch the Show but to keep an eye on Sudipt. He would often be sitting in the second or third row. I'd leave five or six rows and choose a seat from where I could watch both Vandana and Sudipt. All kinds of people would come for the Show. From schoolchildren to the elderly. One old man was always there, sitting in the front row, wearing white, carrying a walking stick. Halfway through the Show, his head would start drooping. There was a young woman who would suddenly smile while listening, then immediately bend her head and start scribbling in her notebook.

As soon as the lights started dimming, a small circle of light would illuminate the pages fluttering in Vandana's hands and her voice would slowly rise: '… The picture of discontentment in the lane, where everyone lifts their feet so that he can run from where he is standing …!' All through the Show, she would keep her eyes downcast as she gave voice to the text. She would raise her eyes only for a few seconds. That's when I felt she was looking at him. He, who must have been the first to come and sit in the hall only to look at Vandana, he, who I had come to keep an eye on as I sat crouching in one of the last rows – I, who would get lost, without wanting to, in the labyrinth of beauty that Vandana's chosen works evoked.

As soon as Vandana would start reading the last passage, I would quietly get up and leave, embarrassed that I was returning after spying on a good, decent man; irritated with myself that once again I had found nothing, nothing at all, not even a fragment to uphold my fears; uneasy that Noa might have got late getting home; wondering if Lakhna had gone to pick her up at the right time or not. As I walked down the street with my head bent, I would sense that everyone was looking at me from the corners of their eyes and suppressing their laughter, and that is when I would feel a light radiating in the darkness within me, just like the glow surrounding Vandana's hands and the pages they held. A part of my mind would suddenly brighten up. In fact, a little ripple of light would start floating about in a small part of my mind. Transparent fibres of joy would rise from some unseen corners of my being, overwhelm my mind and, almost swimming in them, I would keep walking on the side of the road. I would arrive home. Lakhna would be sitting drowsily at the door, waiting for my permission to go pick up Noa from the playground.

The river flows near the hall. After the rains, people go fishing there. During those days, when the courtyard is quiet, you can hear the rustling of the river, as if it has crept closer.

Kishore

It's not as if we didn't try to stop it. It's not as if we just sat around, silently watching everything. And it's not as if we gave them the slightest encouragement. We got to know late. Or should I say we realised the gravity of the situation late. Though which decent person would call what happened serious or grave! It's not that we began our inquiries late. We didn't begin our inquiries late. We were alert from the beginning. We have been raised like that, so we were alert from day one. From the day he first came to our house on some pretext. No, not on any pretext – he came because I had invited him. Who will believe that it was I who asked him to come home. Who will believe that a sharp, cautious person like me would do something like this. I was the one who invited him. I was the one who drew his attention to me, which led to their meeting.

I often went to his library. Especially when it was very hot. The whole city would be sweltering in the hot sun, and my skin would feel as if it was plotting against my own body. Instead of a usual summer, it was a season of burning heat. Everything was smouldering everywhere. The tar on the naked roads melted off the raised part in the middle and trickled towards the sides. It was as difficult for cars to drive down the road as it was for pedestrians to walk on them. The footpath was dotted with laburnum trees whose yellow flowers, like little cold suns, gave some relief. On such days, when every moment in the afternoon seemed to drip melted iron on my head, I would first cover the entrance of the shop with a white sheet, after which there would be a short respite, but very soon this solution would stop working. The hot, bright sun would skirt the white sheet and find other ways to enter the shop through various cracks and openings. There was only one building near the bazaar that was open to all and whose thick walls made of limestone kept it cool. This was the city's largest library. It wasn't far from the shop. When the heat of May became unbearable, I would leave the shop open and step out, and burnt by the loo, braving the now still, now swirling wind and almost dizzy from the heat, I would walk to the library. To enter the library, you had to go to the first floor of the building. You had to cross two verandahs to get there. Entering the verandahs, I would leave behind the searing heat of May, and cold, musty, still air – the sort you find in old, damp buildings – would envelop me from all sides. After crossing the verandahs, there was a wide flight of stone steps and, still in the grip of some residual unconsciousness from the heat outside, I would almost float up the stairs, faltering every now and then, as if I could actually taste the cold while climbing. After passing by two closed doors, there would be a third door, a big, open door, and as soon as you reached it, you would see racks full of books stretching into the distance. Pale light from the lamps above the racks would fall on the books like drizzle. As if I had arrived at the shore of a sea of heat, I would walk with heavy steps towards the long table inside and sit, or rather collapse, into one of the chairs arranged around it. Oblivious to the people around me, oblivious to the books. The heightened heat in my body would slowly abate, and I'd feel myself cooling down.

This was his library.

This was where he would sit, in a small chamber behind the racks, surrounded by books. There was always some book or the other in his hands. His eyes would be looking down at the book, slowly moving over the page. The fan ruffled his tousled hair. It was here, on one such summer afternoon, that I met him. When I made the mistake that I never should have. Here. Right here. In this hall full of books. He would often stroll out of his chamber and, without looking at anyone, go out through the open door. After walking out, he would put his hand inside his pocket, take out a packet of cigarettes and, standing in the long, wide verandah in front of the library, strike a match and then, looking into the distance, light a cigarette. And if someone called out to him, he would leave his burning cigarette on the balcony grille and immediately rush inside.

After sitting in the coolness of the library for a while, I would start looking around. Sometimes picking up a book lying on the table and flipping through its pages. Sometimes opening a magazine and reading it at random. I always felt that at any moment he would ask me what I was doing there, since I never read anything. When I was a child, our maternal grandfather used to take us to the new park that had just opened in the city. We would wait all day to go there. But I would feel the gardener's eyes on me no matter where I went. As if I was going to commit the exact mistake the gardener was lying in wait for. The attraction of the park mixed with my fear of the gardener dragged on for who knows how many days. Perhaps it was the same fear that now followed me to the library. Once born, it never goes away. Old things stick to new situations, coming to the fore again and again. It converts the library into the park, the librarian into a gardener. Otherwise, why did that fear seem so familiar on those hot afternoons spent in the library. Turning the pages of a book or magazine, pretending to read, I would wait for the afternoon to wane. If something caught my interest, I would read it for a bit. That is how I was quite shaken when I read about Gandhi ji's views on the Bihar earthquake. How did Gandhi ji see a connection between untouchability and the shaking of the ground? Who knows what a powerful being such as him might see? Sometimes feeling drowsy, I would put my head down on the book and sleep for two to three hours. I kept feeling that he knew I didn't come here for the books but for the cool, that is why, every time he passed me by after smoking his cigarette, there would be a thin smile on his face. Not just that, he would deliberately ask me about my saffron business. Even when I would grab hold of a book, hold it tightly in my hands and stare at some sentence as soon as I saw him coming close.

'So, Kishore bhai, have you got any new saffron?'

'No! Did you want any?'

'No, I was just asking.'

He was just asking. Why was he just asking? Didn't I know why he was just asking. I know he wanted to remind me that I was a trader. No, not a trader, but a small-time trader. But, Mr Sudipt, wherever you are now, listen to me, listen to me carefully. There is nothing demeaning about running a business. Why, is it something demeaning? Moreover, I am not running a business of selling jaggery, I am running a business of selling saffron. It is famous all over the world, it is the pride of Kashmir. No matter what anyone may think, I do business in saffron, and I will continue doing business in saffron.

On those burning summer afternoons, I genuinely tried, many times, to look inside books, but after reading a few sentences, my attention would wander. I couldn't understand what I was reading, nor how it was relevant or useful to my life. Perhaps books don't open their doors and windows for some people. No matter how hard they knock, they can't enter the books. But is it the fault of those people? They are simply made that way. I am simply made that way. How is it my fault? In which case, why did he laugh at me? He who thought of himself as so educated and intelligent. By all rights, he should have asked God, 'Why is Kishore bhai kesarwallah like this?' How is it my fault? It is God's doing that I am the way I am.

Yes, I did make one mistake. When I knew he riled me so much, why did I, in that fateful moment, invite him to come home? Why? I needn't have invited him. Perhaps I thought that if I got to know him a little better, I wouldn't be on tenterhooks when hanging around the library uselessly. He would no longer be just a librarian, but a librarian who was indebted to me. Or maybe at that moment I felt I wanted to be in the vicinity of educated people. Or maybe, by bringing him close to me, I wanted, just for my own satisfaction, to stifle the aura that surrounded him. I don't know why I invited him home.

Sitting for quite a while in the stale air of the library, I first composed a sentence in my mind. I chiselled it into shape, then, timidly, with scared steps, went towards Sudipt's chamber. For a moment I did think I should let it be, but as I hesitated, he came out of the chamber, one hand holding an extinguished cigarette, the other rummaging in his pocket for a matchbox. Seeing me, he stopped. Pushing aside my dithering, I uttered the sentence I had prepared with so much effort a few minutes ago:

'Will you come to my place to eat?'

Even after so much preparation, I couldn't say it right. The sentence I had formed in my mind was 'Would you like to come to my home for a meal?' but I said something else entirely. He didn't miss a beat at my lapse, smiled lightly and said, 'Of course. You'll give me saffron milk to drink, won't you?'

‘Only when you see the Show will you understand the pleasure of coming here.’ A boy had brought his friend there for the first time. She looks at the people going up the stairs.

Vandana

It was him.

Stooping a little, he was rattling the door chain. For a long time it seemed.

I was strolling on the terrace.

The sky was transparent in its blueness, where countless birds flew, long streaks of their path of flight floating behind them.

The sun was about to set. The western sky was turning pale red and gold.

Every evening was a new colour. Every day I would try to guess what colour the evening would be.

That evening, too, on the open terrace, I was waiting for the still air to take on a colour.

From afar, I could hear the rattling of the door chain.

In the twilight, even my own voice seemed to come from far away. It was the chain on the door of our house. Unconcerned, I kept strolling on the terrace, busy watching the changing formations of the birds in the sky.

Once again, the noise of the rattling chain filled my ears. This time it sounded quite close to me.

I leaned over the parapet of the roof. As I did so, my hair, tied in a braid, slid off my shoulder and swung down.

He was standing in front of the closed door.

The comb stuck at the end of my plait fell off. Right in front of him. He lifted his head. There was a thin smile on his face. He saw me and then looked down again. Picking up the comb, he said softly, 'Does Kishore babu stay here?'

The words were stuck in my throat. I looked at his face, at the comb in his hands, then, from the corner of my eye, at my long, dangling black plait. As if it was as confused and nervous as I was, just hanging there, motionless. Somehow, I got the words out: 'Please wait, I am coming.'

As I straightened after saying this, I found the fibres of air around me had turned a pale rosy colour. As if they had been waiting for me to lean over before changing colour. For a while, I stood on the terrace, dazed and dumbstruck. I felt as if the wings of the flying birds were emitting a chhap-chhap sound. Was the evening intent on taking the colour from my cheeks, now reddening with shyness, and spreading it everywhere! Was the colour of my embarrassment going to overwhelm the entire city! I thought I had lingered there too long. I hurried to the stairs. I quickly went down and opened the door.

He was standing in front of me. Pushing the hair back from his forehead, he held out the comb and said in a soft voice, 'At least you didn't follow the same route as your comb!'

I all but snatched the comb from him. I turned and was about to go when it occurred to me that our guest was still standing at the door. When I turned back, there was a suppressed smile on his face.

'You take care of your comb. Don't worry about me. I'll wait a little longer.'

Without giving him a proper look, I said, 'Please come sit inside. My uncle will soon be here.'

I began clearing the newspapers lying around on the chairs. It didn't even occur to me that the room was in darkness. He whispered, 'Let the newspapers be, I'll remove them. I do this every day. Please switch on the light.'

Mechanically, I grabbed at the switch. The room filled with yellow light. Without glancing at him, I left the room. I started running and stopped only when I reached the kitchen. Ma was holding a glass of water. She held it out to me. Strange things were happening. I took the glass and, looking into her eyes, tried to figure out what I was supposed to do with it.

'Some friend of Kish's has come, and I don't know where Biddu is. You go and give this to him.'

I turned and went back to the room I had just left, where he sat, drenched in yellow light. Seeing the glass, he laughed and said gently, 'I didn't want the comb nor the water. Nevertheless, it's good of you to give me some water.'

Once again, I was flustered. Placing the glass on a corner stool, I sat on the sofa, the tray still in my hands. I kept looking at the door from the corner of my eye. Once my uncle came, I could hand over our guest to him and be on my way. Hand him over to my uncle! The same uncle who, in the days to come, would thirst for this guest's blood, who would do all he could to tear this guest away from me. Uncle, when will you understand that to make people meet, all that chance does is free up time to create an opportune moment, leave it undisturbed and then, hiding behind a curtain, watch whether the two people are moving towards each other or not – and if they really are, then leaving behind a whiff of its presence, it steps aside. And in all this, everyone does their bit, everyone, even those customers who came to buy saffron just when you were about to shut your shop.

'What are you reading these days?'

Yes, he was asking me. Me, who had made a series of awkward mistakes ever since he arrived. I didn't understand what he was asking me. What am I reading? Or studying? Or where am I studying? I am not studying anywhere. I have finished studying. Why should I study or read anything now? I have scaled the mountain that studying was for me, and now I am expected to talk about it once again! That episode is over now. Who is he to ask me, 'What are you reading these days?' No, no, no, nothing. What is happening to me? Why am I thinking such things about someone I don't even know? He has done nothing wrong by asking me this question. Should he have asked me to name the President of Peru? Why am I vexed? Why, why this irritation?

'I have finished my college education.'

'What did you study?'

Oh, he has spoken again. Oh God, why is this man after me? Why doesn't Kish uncle come soon and get me out of here. Why is he asking me so many questions? Is he going to give me a job? Girls don't work in our family. My father's older brother, my tau ji, his daughter once had a job, and he went crazy explaining this to everyone. First, she studied, then worked at a job. Goodness. No one could bear it. The way everyone went after her. People in the family are scared to even talk about what happened to her. Why is this man asking me all this. He has nothing to do with me, yet he is firing away question after question. Why can't his majesty just sit quietly!

'I studied literature.'

Now why did I say that. Why am I telling him all this? He is just firing these questions to pass time. Why should I tell him anything in fact? Why, why, why?

'That's wonderful. What are you reading these days?'

Oh, again a question! Is he a man or a machine for spitting out questions? I don't want to answer his questions. I simply don't want to. I will be quiet. Absolutely quiet. Soon his majesty will himself understand that I don't want to talk. 'So, you thought of me as a machine for spitting out questions,' he said to me in the days that came later. 'Obviously. You kept asking me anything you wanted!'

'What else could I have talked to you about? Should I have instead asked your opinion of the Vedantic doctrine of the unity of Brahma and the individual self?'

'I'm not reading anything these days,' I blurted out, unable to stop myself. What is happening to my tongue. It has been running away on its own. It is saying things I don't want to say to anyone. Least of all to someone like him. But why? What has he done that I am so cross with him? Isn't it enough that he is a machine for spitting out questions.

'What? You're not reading anything? How is that possible? How can anyone who has read literature once survive without reading? I can't believe it. It is a different matter if you don't want to tell me, but I can't believe that someone who got a taste of literature even once can decide to forego that pleasure. No, no, how is it possible? How, how?'

More than to me, he was saying all of this to himself. I was a little scared. What had I said to get him mumbling and muttering like this. I felt I had hurt him with what I had said. Had my words challenged some deeply held belief of his, and he was mumbling now in an effort to deal with its impact. 'Honestly, you really scared me that day; I thought I had scraped at some wound of yours. Is that what happened?'

'I don't remember what happened to me. Perhaps I was so provoked because of Veena. After my separation from her, the only thing I had faith in was literature – I thought it would never abandon me. That not only would it always be with me but also bring the moments I had spent with Veena closer to me. Perhaps when you said that to me I felt that I could no longer depend on literature either. Even literature could forsake me. Who could I trust then? There was nothing left that a person could always rely on.'

'You know, I got so scared by all your mumbling and muttering that I hurriedly lied to you.'

'Actually, I'm reading Dostoevsky's story "White Nights" these days.'

Just in time, I remembered the book I had bought at a college book fair without any thought, which I had put on my table and hadn't bothered to turn a single page. The dismay on his face cleared up a little as soon as he heard the name of the book. Only a remnant of it remained in his knitted brows, like the smile on Alice's amazing Cheshire Cat. Then a kind of delight emerged from deep within him, spreading all over his face. The shine returned to his eyes.

'You're reading Dostoevsky, that too "White Nights". You're diving into the cold waters of sorrow and pain. Oh, what a story! Let me tell you a strange thing about it. When I first read it, I liked one particular simile very much – it stayed in my memory – where the hero of the story takes the hands of a girl waiting for her lover into his own hands, and he feels like he's holding little balls of wool. Hands as soft as balls of wool! I was enchanted by that simile for many days. But when I read the story again, I couldn't find it. I read the story for a third time and still couldn't find it. I was bewildered, after all, where had I imagined those hands that were as soft as balls of wool. Where? Then one day I remembered. When I was immersed in "White Nights", lost in it day and night, I had touched Veena's hands for the first time by the side of the Seine River, and they'd felt like balls of wool to me. Unbeknownst to me, perhaps that soft touch became linked to "White Nights" and I began thinking I had found that touch soft as wool, within the story. I often think that every beautiful story carries empty spaces within it, which we fill with the colours of our experiences. A reader can only be someone who has the strength to pour himself into a story and take on the risk of completing it, who can face the danger of confronting his own life within it. But who knows how all this happens? What do you think?'

Lost in himself, he spoke like that for a while. His hands rose in the air, as if he was trying to hold on to some thought.

'Why were you looking at me and talking without a pause that day?' I asked him later.

'I couldn't take my eyes off you! There was a mosquito on your left cheek.'

I peered inside myself. All the irritation he had caused before had changed into glimmers of respect for him.

There was the sound of the gate opening outside. I looked up and peeked at the door. Kish uncle had come.

'Who is Veena?' The words came out of my mouth.

Before he could answer, Kish uncle opened the door.

The dog ambled into the courtyard. Someone said, 'There's a dog.' Someone else said placidly, 'He lives here. Wait and see, he'll go and sprawl near a flower bed now.'

Biddu

All my life I'll regret that the wretch didn't die at my hands. The bastard never gave me a chance. He died like a petty thief in some corner. No, not like a thief, like a dog. If he had been found lying in a gutter, I would have been even more satisfied. I heard that when they did the postmortem, they found his stomach was empty. He died on an empty stomach, so his ghost will haunt the sweet shops. If he had died with Vando, we would have been rid of this calamity. If the whore had also died, this whole chapter would have come to an end. Now she is sitting on the terrace with her sad face, mourning his death. She is mourning the death of the family's enemy. I told Pita ji so many times not to let this witch get an education. Teach her housework and get rid of her by the time she turns seventeen. All this traipsing off to college every day isn't proper. But no, he went around telling the world that you couldn't find such an educated girl within miles of our village. He was so proud of it, proud of her education. Now handle the situation; forget a few miles, go and find a girl with such shameful traits within a hundred miles of our village. Go, find someone who has shamed her father, her family, the way this girl has. But no, he never listened. No matter how much you tried to make him understand, he didn't listen. He ensured that she was educated and literate, while he went on an endless pilgrimage. It wasn't enough that it was family members who gave her the licence to make such a tamasha of herself.

What a tamasha. And this licence that was given to her, wah. Was this house short of money that we allowed her to do this tamasha? Besides, where was the money in it? She must have spent her own money. You can't put up these things without money, can you? Or maybe some money did come in and that bastard nicked it. I told her so many times, nicely and lovingly, 'Vando, why do you keep doing this? Does it behove a girl from a good family to do all this? Why do you want to get into this mess? What will you get from it?' And what does she say to this? 'Bhaiyya, why do you think like this? You know, a very big French writer does a similar show. There is a fellow feeling among different literary works and concepts, and I want to understand this feeling and bring the works closer to each other as if introducing two unknown people to each other, bas, that's all I do. If you don't understand this, what can I do.' (What is happening to me … I remember Vando's words verbatim – 'literary works', 'concepts', 'fellow feeling' – how has all this stayed in my mind? In fact, how did it get into my head in the first place? I'll have to go to a doctor and get my head cleaned up.) Then she had said, 'You won't understand because you don't want to understand.'

It's true, why should I understand, what's it to me? But why won't I understand? Have I just bummed around all my life that I won't understand your French writer's exploits? That same asshole must have taught you these airs and affectations, and you got snared in that bastard's trap. Tell me, what great things did your French firangi accomplish by doing his tamasha? Did he become a millionaire, a billionaire? Did he buy a mansion in London? That bastard, he spun an international web to trap unwary women. Someone's weaving it in France, someone in America, someone in …

That is why I say it is good that the wretch died, otherwise he would have come up with some new trap. It is in the nature of such people. Catch someone here, catch someone there. They don't let anyone live their life properly. They live happily but make other people miserable. These scoundrels go around pretending to be big thinkers. He was a third-rate librarian, that too, of a dirty, rotting library. And what fantasies. French writers, if you please. Bravo, French writer! Did that French writer save you from dying a dog's death? Tell me, tell me with your dead tongue, did he save you? I only know one thing – death matches one's deeds! You reap as you sow, brother. No one just gets away. You seize an innocent girl, who doesn't belong to you, and think no one will notice. Wah! How can that be. God, the Supreme Being, isn't sitting around swatting flies. He has his eye on everyone. You close the door to your room here and up there, his TV comes on. Everything is being watched there, nothing is left out or forgotten. Everyone's intentions and deeds are being taped, and people are being disposed of accordingly.

Vando, you too will have to reap the fruits of what you've sowed. Someday, if not today. I must have told Kishore uncle twenty-five times to let me deal with these two. Let me. But he too goes around as if he is the most intelligent person there ever was. He said he would discreetly fix everything at home. Now do it discreetly. He made a grand exit but left smearing our faces with shit. Where can we hide? Is there a box we all can huddle inside? Go on now, go and fix everything discreetly. We should have grabbed his daughter in the beginning; the asshole would have caved in in a second. Or we could have broken his leg. But no, apparently, we are better than that, we are very sensible. Arre, Vando's leg was ours, wasn't it? Why didn't we break that? But no, you're too clever aren't you. Now what will you do with all this cleverness? Everyone thinks we have killed him when we haven't done anything. We didn't do it, but we are being blamed for it. This whole mess could have been sorted out right at the beginning. Right when we forbade Vando from leaving the house. We should have been more vigilant back then. We should have put the witch under lock and key. But no, we are decent people. How can we lock our daughter in her room. Arre, if you can forbid her from leaving the house, if you can put a lock on her phone, what is the harm in also locking her in her room? How long would she have sat there with a long, sad face? Being stuck in one room would have brought her back to her senses. Otherwise, why didn't we consider throwing acid on that witch's face. Here's her burnt face, Mr Librarian, why don't you declare your love for her now! If Kish uncle had agreed, there would have been no problem. We could have soaked a towel with acid and, the minute we had a chance, rubbed it on her fair hide. It is only hide, nothing very important. Even if it had burnt, so what, at least her soul would have been saved, the soul that only French writers can penetrate.

No one stares at anyone. Everyone just looks at each other as if to say, 'We've come to meet you too.'

Mridula

I had thought then that Kishore Lal Kothari was right. Their reputation was suffering because of this. If some people that I know start talking to each other the minute they see me, I think it is because of Sudipt; either they are making fun of me or they are pitying me. Somehow, I try to stay calm. There can be many reasons why two people get close to each other. How can Sudipt's closeness to someone else affect his attachment to me. I never saw anything in Sudipt's eyes to suggest there was distance between him and me. Even so, because of the people around me, I began denying my own feelings, and the truth got clouded in the fog of rumours. I could no longer see the truth of my closeness to him. Once again leaving me uneasy. Kishore bhai phoned me often. Without telling me his name. Why did he call me anonymously? Maybe because that is how he could give me street gossip. But I recognised him every time. Not so much from his voice as from the quivering notes of anxiety and pretence. Even then, I would speak to him as if he was someone from the nearby lane. He tried to scare me about Sudipt in all kinds of ways. Often there was a faint threat in his voice. I would just listen to him. Listen and put the phone down. Gradually, he figured out that I knew who he was. One day, Kishore bhai himself tore aside the veil of anonymity and told me his name when he called me. 'Mridula ji, if you want to prevent your home from being destroyed, meet me once.' Before I could say yes, he told me the name of a restaurant in the western part of the city that was only open in the afternoons. Small-time traders went there for lunch and businesspeople for their tea.

As the sun climbed high in the sky, I set off from home. Sudipt had already left for the library. The sharp sun enveloped every little part of my sari-clad body in yellow flames. It was only when I was almost burning from the heat that I realised I had forgotten to bring an umbrella. I immediately turned back. I felt a little relieved. I felt a sense of peace in going back. Now I wouldn't go to meet Kishore bhai. Who knows, something untoward might happen. But I had to save my home, the same home I was feeling so relieved to go back to. Taking my umbrella, I went out again.

I was trembling all the way. I kept darting glances here and there to see if I could spot anyone I knew. Walking down the narrow lane, as I neared the restaurant, I saw a big crowd outside. I instantly turned to go back. I had barely walked a few steps when I saw Kishore bhai coming towards me. I pretended I hadn't seen him, thinking I would give him the slip. If someone saw me in this crowd, what would they think? I had heard that Kishore bhai went around abusing Sudipt, and if people saw me with him, what would they think? No, no, I didn't want to meet Kishore Lal Kothari. I was fine as I was. I was not going to join hands with anyone to do anything against Sudipt. That would be petty and mean. If he finds out, he won't say anything, he will keep quiet, but I would never be able to meet his eyes again. And I would lose the one happiness in my life. When he looks at me, something between love and respect flickers in his gaze. It is difficult to define, but I sense it deep inside me, and I continue to feel it even now. I all but ran past him. Chalo, I escaped, I thought and quickened my stride. My sari kept getting entangled in my legs as I walked ahead with quick steps. I had just walked, rather, run, a short distance when I heard a voice behind me.

'Mridula ji …'

I froze. I was rooted to the ground. As if I had been caught stealing. For a moment my feet turned lifeless as I stood in that narrow little lane. When I turned slowly, fearfully, I found Alim standing in front of me. My panic settled a little, I felt the blood come back to my feet, and I smiled, a smile that came from the depths of my being. Alim assisted Sudipt in the library. He used to say that he worked in the library so that he could read a lot, but he didn't plan to stay on there like Sudipt. He wanted to get a prestigious job in the government.

Sudipt would tease him. 'You are going to leave your regal work in the library to do the clerical work of a collectorate. That is why you are milking my library for all its worth. Here you are the king of books, there you will become the slave of files. Sir, a library is not an ordinary place. Hundreds and millions of worlds lie hidden in such a small space. Open any book and a distinctive world will come alive before you. And invite you to enter. Alim miyan, you will quit ruling over such a kingdom and ruin your life collecting taxes? Do you call this passion?'

Many times I had wanted to question Alim about Vandana and Sudipt, but he was an intelligent young man who held the deepest respect for Sudipt and therefore held me in regard too. Every time he would deflect my queries in such a way as though he was protecting me from falling into the morass of this line of inquiry. A leather bag slung over his shoulder, he was carrying a few books, which he now held out to me, saying, 'I had to give these books to sir. But it will take me a while to get there. If you could take them with you, it would be great, otherwise ...'

Before he could finish, I said, 'Of course, I can take them.'

Alim took out a plastic carry bag from his leather bag, put three or four books into it and handed it to me. No sooner had I taken the books and set off for home than someone called out from behind. This time it was Kishore Lal. He came up to me. He was wearing a light blue shirt and pyjamas. He was smiling as if he had scored some sort of victory.

'Namaste, Mridula ji. How come you are in this part of town today?'

His smile was close to a laugh by now. My heart started beating fast. I could feel it till the tips of my fingers. Alim was on one side, Kishore Lal on the other. I couldn't turn either way. Suppose Alim told Sudipt about this? But what could be done now? I had agreed to meet Kishore Lal here. He was pretending as if we had met by accident. He needn't have done that. Whatever it was, he genuinely wanted this awkward moment to be smoothed over. But was it a problem for him too?

'How are you, Kishore bhai? Do you know Alim?'

I drew his attention to Alim though he had already seen him.

'Of course. He works with Sudipt ji in the library. I have often seen him there. How are you, Alim miyan?'

Alim looked at him, seemingly lost in thought. Perhaps he was aware of his antics. Or perhaps it was only because he hardly knew Kishore Lal. His face looked a little tense. He answered softly, as if he was talking not to Kishore Lal but to himself. 'I'm fine. I will be off now, Mridula ji!'

Passing by the restaurant, he went off towards the part of the city that had the mountains. I kept looking at him till he disappeared from view.

'Come, let's sit down,' Kishore Lal whispered.

Holding the carry bag full of books, I mechanically followed him to the restaurant. It was more of an eatery. There were only a few people there, chatting over chai or coffee. Perhaps just us. As soon as I entered, I began feeling nauseous: all around me was the smell of vegetables, dals, chutneys and pickles.

Kishore Lal walked ahead of me. He appeared unaffected by the all-pervasive smell. Like a real businessman, he cared for nothing except the business at hand, no sight or smell bothered him. And we both knew what this business was. If I wanted, I could have turned back even then. I did want to, but it was as if I no longer had any control over my feet. In the grip of some unknown fear, I thought my body was behaving strangely.

'Please sit, Mridula ji!'

Gesturing towards a table close by, Kishore Lal sat down in a corner chair. There was a newspaper lying on the empty chair in front of him. I removed it and sat down. I put the carry bag of books on the chair next to me. My anxiety was intensifying. Then I heard him say, 'What will you have?'

As soon as he spoke, a waiter wearing grubby clothes, with an even dirtier towel draped over one shoulder, materialised next to us. The entire day's tiredness was accumulated in the drops of sweat on his face.

'Anything!' I said.

I didn't hear what he said to the waiter. By now, the blood was pounding so loud and fast in my ears that I could only hear snatches of what was being uttered, as if a few words, like thin shards stuck to the edges of my heartbeats, were floating to my ears. Dhak dhak dhak dhak. 'Nothing is hidden from you, dhak dhak dhak,' Kishore bhai was saying. Dhak dhak dhak dhak. 'Somehow please stop all this, dhak dhak dhak dhak.' 'What are you dhak dhak dhak dhak referring to?' Dhak dhak. 'Don't you dhak dhak know, dhak dhak?' I could hear Kishore Lal's dull voice from behind my thudding heartbeats. As if it was coming from behind some billowing curtains, reaching me after scattering in every direction. Dhak dhak dhak dhak. 'Mridula ji, we are getting a bad name, I mean, dhak dhak, your reputation is also suff … dhak dhak dhak dhak dhak.' 'What can I do dhak dhak dhak? You should … dhak dhak dhak.' 'I will be very strict dhak dhak with Vandana dhak dhak dhak. After all, she is dhak dhak my niece dhak dhak.' 'You shouldn't let her dhak dhak your home dhak dhak dhak dhak.'

I was constantly looking around me. The people sitting at the dozen-odd tables near us were bent over their food-laden plates. Right next to us, a woman was eating slowly from her steel plate, and the two children, a boy and a girl, sitting in front of her were eating with their hands and dropping vast quantities of food. 'Why don't you say something dhak dhak dhak … to Sudipt … dhak dhak. He's such an exceptional man … dhak dhak dhak dhak … why is he stuck in … dhak dhak … mess.' I thought Alim had entered the restaurant from behind me. By then the waiter had placed our cups of tea on the table. I quickly scooped up the carry bag and stood up.

'If you want then Su … p … dhak … ji… dhak dhak dhak dhak.' The next instant I was all but running to the door. My sari was getting entangled in my swiftly moving feet. Dhak dhak dhak dhak. Dhak dhak dhak dhak. Dhak dhak I was running. Dhak dhak dhak dhak I almost stopped hearing Kishore Lal's voice from behind me. Now it was just my heartbeats, sounding like falling raindrops, that I heard all around me. It felt like I was passing through a downpour of my own heartbeats. I hurried out of the door.

I practically ran all the way back. Reaching home, I fell on the bed with a thud, as if my body had just been pierced by arrows from all sides.

The next day Vandana was forbidden from leaving the house. In a way I had wanted this to happen, but I didn't feel as happy as I should have. It wasn't that I felt no happiness at all. I did. For a moment I felt I would be free of this complication in my life. The shadow of doubts and misgivings that hovered between us would be gone. I had drawn back a little from him lately, now I would be able to get close, much closer to him. And he to me. I believed this, at least for a while, I absolutely believed it. Actually I had had nothing to do with what had happened, not at all. I wouldn't dream of doing such a thing or getting it done, but a fuzzy feeling of contentment had permeated my mind so intensely, it was as if a personal mission had been accomplished. Then I was just beginning to understand that there is no relationship that can be mended by removing someone from the scene. This is the difference between objects and people: objects, once removed, stay removed, but a person who has been removed occupies the space they vacated even more fully. You may not see them, but they are there, and when you reach out to the space vacated by them, you feel them even more intensely than you did before.

With Vandana's house arrest, Sudipt was devastated. His face, hands, movements exhibited abject helplessness. He never spoke much, but now he fell completely silent. Cigarette between his lips, he paced his room with heavy steps, as if he was inside a cage. Maybe he had doubts about my role in all this. How could I tell him that I had fled before I could do anything. How could I defend myself from an allegation that hadn't been made in the first place? He was sinking, fast, somewhere far away. Like a star that had slipped from its orbit and was lost in the emptiness of space. The Sudipt we could see was but a shadow, left behind by the Sudipt who was lost nobody knew where.

I would call him to eat, and he would look at me as if he couldn't process what I had said. After I would call out to him, he would stare out of the window as if he was calling himself back for a short while from some faraway place. Noa seemed to understand this. During those days, she tried to address all her queries to herself, fill her pen with ink on her own, cover her notebooks by herself, and she tried to leave Sudipt alone.

On the evening of the Show, Sudipt didn't come back from the library the way he used to after the Show was over. His footsteps would sound in the courtyard of the house sometime after Vandana finished her Show. I was worried. I ran to the library. The evening was drawing to a close. The rays of the dying sun swept over the library roof. I could hear my footsteps as I climbed the stairs. The library was empty. Of the chairs arranged around the long table, two were pulled back and stood a little askew. Perhaps two visitors had left them like that, and Sudipt had gone away without noticing them.

Where could he have gone?

Where should I look for him?

I didn't have much time. I had to get home soon. Lakhna would be waiting for me so he could go and pick up Noa. And Noa would be waiting for Lakhna. Suppose everyone else had left and she was alone? My anxiety increased. Where could he have gone? At first, I thought I was worrying unnecessarily. But deep inside, I felt the same way one would feel if they were looking for a sick person who had left his sickbed and gone off somewhere. He wasn't sick. He had gone to the library this morning. Had he stopped somewhere? Or had someone stopped him? They might hurt him. Or an accident could be arranged. How difficult was it to engineer an accident for someone walking on the street, their head buried in an open book? Could they stoop so low? Who knows? Why was I thinking all this? Is it so easy to hurt or injure somebody? Why not? When you can lock up an independent citizen of the country in her home, how hard can it be to orchestrate an accident? No, no, how can anyone be so cruel? What had Vandana done that you took away her freedom like this? I? No, not I. I didn't lock her up. I was only trying to save my home, a home made up of delicate wisps of snow. I was trying to keep Noa secure, I was trying to prevent Sudipt from tarnishing his reputation. But was I truly doing this? Ufff, what did I end up doing? Even if it was for a few moments, I had stooped so low. How could I come out of this? I couldn't see any way out. How could I come out of this? Should I tell Vandana everything; she will understand my plight. Will she forgive me? Even if she doesn't, at least I will feel lighter. But how will I reach Vandana? How? She's confined to her room. A whirlwind of questions swirled within me as I was passing by the hall where Vandana held her Show. I purposely tried to avoid looking there. Normally, this hall would be resounding with her recitation of a unique combination of exceptional extracts from a variety of literary works. Members of the audience would be holding their breath, listening to the shifting cadences in Vandana's voice. But right now, the place was completely quiet and peaceful. The last light of the evening was fading. Some leaves on the trees in the front, dancing in the still air, were falling to the ground. From the corner of my eye, I sensed rather than saw a silent shape standing still inside the gate leading to the hall, in front of the hall's door. Startled, I turned to look. Sudipt was standing there, facing the door. The gate was slightly ajar. The dim, fading light was falling on the gate and on his slightly stooped back, from where it seemed to slide down. One foot was on a lower stair and the other at a slight angle on the stair above. Not as if he was climbing the stairs, but as if that was as far as he would go. Both his hands were on his cheeks but resting lightly, as if they had stopped there for a moment, hesitating, on their way to touching something else. I looked at him for some time. Then, I don't know what came over me that I went behind him and put my hand on his shoulder. He turned around with lightning speed, but seeing me, sagged visibly. His face was wet, and his red eyes seemed buried beneath a veil of countless tears. Anyone could drown in so many tears. Just about anyone. I don't know what I am made of, that I kept floating on the surface of his agony, and I remain standing on that shore till today, though Sudipt's boat has quietly left and sailed far away into the distance.

The sunshine is slowly sliding up to the top of the tall neem tree in the courtyard. As if the flood of warm sunshine is ebbing away, leaving behind a place for darkness. Unlike the breeze. The breeze shakes the branches and leaves of the neem every now and then, all the way from top to bottom, before vanishing.

Marg

The novel has reached its halfway mark. Or perhaps a little more or a little less than that. Pausing at this juncture to rest a little, I am lost in thought. Will this novel ever end, or will I have to wait all my life for it to end? It is difficult to know – actually, it is impossible to know. I am told there are some prior signs of when a novel comes to a close, but I don't know anything about them. That is why I am still a poet, not a novelist. And I am a poet only because of my earlier works. Otherwise, I haven't managed to become either a novelist or a poet. I am like a falling star that is lost in the emptiness of the universe of writing. Like a chess player who reaches the middle of the game and, realising that he is sinking, keeps flailing about, trying to save himself.

But there is one question …

I started out with a few pages that I wanted to see transformed into a novel, and I have been wandering around with them for so long that I am no longer bothered whether they will make it into a novel or not. Perhaps I am writing or editing something, again and again, day after day, that which has to be written and edited again and again, day after day. As if I am climbing a mountain. After many days of climbing up and coming down, when I lift my head, I can't see the peak, and I start climbing again. My elderly friend Kavalam used to tell me that his time would be up the day he finished the Malayalam translation of the *Bhagavata Purana*. And that is what happened to him. Year after year, he kept translating the *Bhagavata Purana* and, despite his delicate health, continued doing wonderful theatre. But that translation was destined to finish one day. And it did. About eight months later, his time was up. Was this the fear these pages had? That the moment they were transformed into a novel, they too would be rendered lifeless, and so they kept postponing such an eventuality. Though this fear is not unfounded. After the novel is finished, the pages will be confined between the book covers. They will reawaken only when a reader picks up the book and breathes life into it. Does that really happen? Is that why I am caught in this game of writing and editing? Will I never be able to get through these pages?

There must be a reason why I am continuously writing and editing. There must be something. I am certainly hopeful – or perhaps believe that hope is there, somewhere. I may not be able to see it clearly, but it is surely there. I am hopeful of the hope within me that someday these pages will take the form of a novel. Someday I will reach the summit of this endless mountain, though once I reach there, maybe little will remain of me. Or maybe that won't happen. It might not happen at all, in which case these pages I have been writing for years will end up as loose, scattered sheets. I am hopeful of the hopelessness within me too. But I am not alone in this tussle between hope and hopelessness. There are others with me, let me call them characters. Meaning various presences who walk in a certain way, use their brains, spread their doubts, exude goodwill, deal with their attachments. All in a particular way. I didn't know them from before. I am newly acquainted with them. They're quite new. I didn't know them before they entered these pages, and now, if after living with them on these pages for so many years I know them a little, it is because of their kindness. It has hardly anything to do with me. All I have done is try to understand them, but they know it and so do I that the irony is that no one can understand us fully, finally, once and for all. No one can, unless they attain salvation; however, once they do, they will no longer know us as them, him or her. What they will know is something else altogether. Till the time I am I, you are you, they are they, no one can understand us. I can't even understand myself, nor can you, nor can they.

Then why write a novel at all?

When you can't even understand your characters, why rack your brain over it?

The answer is difficult, but there is an answer. Let me try and explain. Perhaps reading or writing a novel is like wandering around the forest of language with a few characters. The forest of language or the jungle of speech. This is the jungle in which I saw Vandana's tears, Mridula's fear-soaked sense of duty, Kishore Kothari's arrogance, Sneha's loving friendship, Sanvli's astonishing life. It is through them that I met Sudipt. I met that dead character in the forest of language. In the jungle of speech. Like me, they too were wandering around in that jungle, lost. Trying to understand the significance of their existence in the light of death. They were wandering about, lost. Savouring the winter sun, the falling yellow leaves in the summer. Someone would go and sleep in the break between sentences, someone else would park themselves at the semicolon. Sometimes someone would shove aside a full stop like a big, heavy gate that had come in their way and move on to the next sentence.

Whenever I would come face to face with these characters, they always had something to say to me. It may be more appropriate to say that their bodies were made of their voices. They existed in their speech. I would listen without interrupting them. At the same time, I would spread some blank pages below them, the same way a sheet is spread out on the ground for harsingar flowers. The harsingar lying strewn on this sheet will perhaps go on to take the form of a novel. If that doesn't happen, then their fragrance will linger in my room and remind me that for some years I wandered in that jungle of speech, where I saw Vandana searching for a way to keep her memories alive or Mridula dealing with her intense dilemmas or Lakhna staring with amazement at the society around him or Noa slowly opening her eyes while shedding tears of loss or Kishore Kothari steeped in pride at selling saffron …

Not too many elderly people come for the Show. Especially in the winter, when going home, the trembling tendrils of the night would leave their bodies shivering. The street lights are so shrouded in mist that there is always a smudge of pale, wan yellow light below them, which sometimes wobbles in the waves of the night. In such a situation, who can find their way back home?

Sushila

What was Vandana's fault? What did she do that we went after her? That she became friends with Sudipt? Friendship with a man who, if you sat next to him, would make you feel good about your being. Even if for a short while. There was something about the way he spoke that made you unknowingly begin to appreciate things in your life that you had paid no attention to. It was only when he asked me that I remembered, after years, the harsingar tree in the courtyard of my ancestral house, how it used to shed its flowers every day, how I used to sit on a chair below it every morning and the flowers would fall all over me. 'Then you're the daughter of the house of the falling harsingar,' he said to me. This was Sudipt with whom Vandana was friends.

Then why did I join hands with the others in causing her so much pain? Perhaps we can't bear the radiance on our children's faces that hasn't sprung from us. Yes, it was this radiance on Vandana's face, it was the brilliance in her eyes that we couldn't bear; we saw the danger in them and, with all our might, doubled down on ending it. Is it that we human beings, like birds, never learnt how to be parents to our children? Nature had left this small task to us, but we couldn't even do that. We don't even notice when our children grow wings and should be left to their own devices. We have decided that being a mother means making sure your children do the same things that have been happening for ages. You must wrap your children in the same blanket of 'that's how it has always been' so that they stay safe. Even if this safety prevents them from blossoming.

When we were ineffective in doing this, we stopped Vandana from going out. I was the one who told her of our decision. After listening to me, she looked at me with some surprise and fear. And a little pity too. As if she didn't really know me. As soon as I saw her eyes slowly emerge from behind the veil of her eyelashes, I understood that now no one could stop Vandana from distancing herself from us. By trying to imprison her in the house we were breaking whatever little remained of our relationship with her. But who could I have said this to? Kish firmly believed that everything would get fixed once we stopped Vandana from going out.

'Bhabhi, you don't know, the whole town is laughing at us.'

Kish didn't speak like this often. He would usually get busy with accounts once he was back from the shop. He would quietly go and have a bath and then sit down for dinner, his clothes still damp. When he said that, I was shocked. That's when Biddu showed up and, as always, began muttering darkly about how Vandana was painting the town red with Sudipt. As always, instead of saying what he wanted to say clearly, he kept abusing Sudipt and Vandana.

'We should hang the bastard.'

I shushed Biddu and, looking at Kish, asked, 'So what is to be done?'

Kish was silent. As if he was trying to think of a subtle way out of the situation. Just then Vandana walked into the kitchen for something. Kish saw her and through his eyes signalled us to keep quiet. She didn't notice anything amiss and went out with a glass of water. She never suspected that we had assembled there to discuss ways of confining her. Seeing her lost in herself, my eyes welled up, as if I was bidding farewell to something we shared between us. Something that was pure, that whispered and sighed between us without our knowledge, and we sensed it only when it was being violated. A shiver ran through my body. I was afraid that we would be too hard on her, that our restrictions would be too severe. Kish was looking troubled, Biddu as always full of hatred for others, which was born out of his irresponsibility and recklessness. At that moment, this hatred was directed at Sudipt, but since Sudipt was out of his reach, it was shifting towards Vandana. Thinking I should speak, I said, 'Let's stop her from doing the Show.'

Biddu jumped up and spat out, 'Nothing will come of asking her not to do the Show. Stop her from going out of the house!'

He spoke with such excessive force that I trembled at the hatred boiling inside him. This is my son! How does he have so much hatred inside him? Surely, Vando must have done something untoward, else why would he talk like this. Kish quickly looked up and glared at Biddu. Biddu went quiet. All of us looked at Kish. As if we had made up our minds that we would do what he said. Kish was deserving of this faith. The shop ran because of his capability. He was the one who had decided some years ago that the saffron business would be more profitable in the city, and we had shifted here overnight. He ran the shop with great dedication. Vando's papa did go and sit in the shop, and his network of contacts no doubt helped the business, but without Kish, none of this would have helped in the smooth running of the shop. He said hesitantly:

'Biddu is an idiot, but what he is saying makes sense. What can we do to the librarian? Let Vandana stay at home. We will make her understand. There is no question of her doing the Show. Bhabhi, you tell her, from tomorrow onwards she will stay inside the house!'

Vandana began staying at home, or rather, in her room. She stepped out only for her meals. Whenever I went to her room, I found her reading. I would keep a glass of saffron milk on her table and leave. Her friend Sneha came to meet her quite a few times. Each time, she was told that Vandana had gone to visit her nani. 'But what about her Show?' she asked. 'Vandana would know, but she hasn't said when she will be back.' How could we know how long we would have to keep Vandana in captivity? Sneha would go away, quite perplexed. I felt she understood what was going on. But she didn't try to dig any further; perhaps she wanted to allow Vandana some dignity, show her the respect she deserved. As for Sudipt's phone calls, I have no idea how they were dealt with. In any case, Sudipt's intangible presence was so overpowering in our house that the idea of talking to him on the phone seemed incongruous. Why would someone who is hovering around you all the time need the phone to talk to you?

Vandana stopped raising her eyes to see me. She hid herself in a shawl. Seeing the embroidered yellow border on her black shawl, you would think she had enhanced the restrictions we had placed on her and shackled herself with a yellow-coloured chain. In spite of it, she was a ripple of sorrow spreading all over the house. I went to her room often. Not once did she look up from her books. The winter sun, pouring in from the window, would caress her head as if apologising to her on our behalf.

Blessed are the limits of our fear that we work like machines towards breaking the shining threads of our relationship with our children. We remain at it, all the time.

The cat's eyes shine on the parapet of the hall's terrace. It stares unblinkingly at the people walking from the courtyard to the stairs. Then, in a leisurely manner, it leaps onto the branch of a nearby tree.

Veena

He went back to his country. I heard he has started working at a library there.

It's been so long since he went away that the pain of his absence has only grown in me. In such a way that if it recedes, I will feel as if a limb from my body has fallen off.

Paris has been forlorn for years now. Did he tell me the story of Shakuntala leaving Rishi Kanva's hermitage to go to King Dushyant's palace for these times? Or was that merely a coincidence? Or a sketch of a future that he – like I – knew nothing about then. After Shakuntala's departure, the hermitage dwellers, her friends, the rishi, all of them felt as if the whole ashram had become forsaken. As if it had emptied out from within. Something similar happened in the American film we went to see at the Odeon Theatre. A late-night show that only film lovers or drunkards or tired, exhausted people came to see. 'I have heard that this director is a little unconventional. Though he is from Hollywood, he makes different kinds of films. Let's see,' he had said while standing in the line for tickets. He always began reading a new book, went to see a new film or entered an art gallery with full enthusiasm. As if he was reading a book or watching a film for the first time in his life. At the end of the film, the taxi driver drops off his girlfriend from the cab for the last time and drives away. The sprawl of New York City is reflected in the rearview mirror, but despite all the lights and glitter, it looks empty and deserted. As though for the taxi driver the whole city has become deserted.

With his going, this bustling city too became empty. Sometimes it did feel crowded, but I knew that beneath the hustle and bustle, an unfathomable emptiness lay panting, and I could fall into it any moment.

I could have also gone back after completing my studies. But gone back to where? To whom? I decided to stay back because I thought I was at least familiar with my loneliness here. I didn't realise that you can rarely get familiar with loneliness. Sometimes it can seem familiar, but that's not always the case. Perhaps it's a mark of loneliness that it reveals its unfamiliar aspect to us every time but hides its familiar side forever, in perpetuity. I spent so many years here in the hope that maybe I would come to know my loneliness. That didn't happen. It continued to pierce me, deep within, and holding on to that pain, I continued running from home to hospital and hospital to home. I would look outside of myself, through the windows of my house or through the eyes of the patients in the hospital. The only relief was passing by those streets where we had walked together or when I touched the shadows of the tall trees where we had sheltered in the rain and he had carefully wiped the water dripping on my forehead with the sleeve of his sweater so that it didn't smudge my bindi – it was then, for a moment, that the faint fragrance of his unseen nearness would rush towards me and spread inside me.

I believe he has named his daughter Noa. Noa! Yes, Noa! That's what my seventeenth-floor apartment is called. Noa! When he came there for the first time, he looked out of the window and said, 'Being here seems like there is no one left in the world except for us. We are the ones who will manage life and take it forward. Veena, is this your home or is it Noah's Ark? The one and only Noah's Ark sailing the sea of the world.' He hasn't forgotten me. Not at all. Perhaps he has quietly hidden the memory of our relationship in his daughter's name. She is his daughter, she is also a remembrance of our closeness.

I tried to stop him from going. But in a way that wouldn't make it evident that I was deliberately trying to hold him back.

'… Here you can do a lot of work in your subject. And isn't that what you want too …'

'… Are there any universities left in India where you can do the kind of work you want …'

'… I think your future is here in Europe. If you go back, your growth might get stalled …'

He didn't listen to me. Not at all. He went away. I was in the middle of my studies and stayed on. I definitely considered going back. But that didn't happen. I just got stuck here. He too never came back. He stayed there and made it his home.

This is the same bridge. Yes, he used to sit on a bench below this bridge with his books open. His head buried in the books for hours. As if the ripples in the water in front of him didn't exist. Or maybe he saw them with an inner eye. (Amazing. The eyes on your face are becoming weak, and you're talking about the inner eye!) A fragmented sky floats on the flowing waters of the Seine in the warm afternoon sunshine. People would cross the wooden bridge on foot. Young men and women would lean on the railing, holding hands and gazing at the water flowing below. I too would look down. I could see him sitting beneath the bridge, but I never paid him much attention. That was the place where I would usually stand and wait.

Jacque used to work for a few hours at a travel company nearby. He would leave in the late evening. I would come away from college an hour or two earlier before he would arrive and spend the time standing on the bridge. The long rays of the setting sun would descend on every lane and alleyway of the city. Some would hide behind the little waves in the flowing water. Every few minutes, spreading these rays on the water, a cruise boat would glide down the Seine and pass under the bridge. I could see him coming from afar. Almost sliding down the sun's lengthening rays, I would fling myself into his arms and cling to him. Our arms entwined, we would cross the bridge, go to a restaurant and tell each other how our day went.

'They're sending me to Senegal,' Jacque said that day, after his office was over. 'Come with me.'

I stayed silent. I couldn't go. There were two years left of my medical school. Jacque knew this very well. He also knew how deeply I was committed to my studies. I had to complete my course. I wanted to learn something new every day. Even if I had wanted to, I couldn't have gone with him.

'I can't go with you,' I said, my eyes almost boring into his.

Looking to my side, as if picking out and throwing my gaze away like a splinter, Jacque said, 'I am not sure when I will be back.'

Letting go of the railing, I straightened up. Giving him a hug, kissing his forehead, I said, 'I will wait till you come back.'

All the blood in his body rushed to his face. He extricated himself from my arms and began walking towards the other side of the bridge. I ran after him, but I slipped and fell. I let out a scream, and blood began to trickle from my upper lip. He continued walking straight ahead. I got up and watched him leave. 'He is angry. He will calm down. I will call him after a while,' I thought and didn't follow him. I called him late at night from the hostel. The phone kept ringing. Maybe he was taking a bath, I thought. I called again after a bit. He didn't pick up. I stood in the bitter cold of the hostel corridor till late at night, calling him. I rushed to his room early in the morning. I got off the Metro and, in a bid to get to him as fast as I could, began running towards his place. The pale early morning light bathed the footpath that was still damp from the night dew. My feet kept slipping on the round iron grilles encircling the bottom of trees that dotted the footpath at regular intervals. I opened the door of the building and dashed up the wooden stairs. Thup-thup-thup-thup. The complete silence inside crumbled like a fine layer of snow. His room was shut. After ringing the bell a few times, I began banging on the door, as if that was the only thing standing between us. Hearing the din, the elderly landlady came out of the adjoining apartment.

'He left the room at night. I am having coffee. Would you like to join me?'

Even after this, I continued going to the bridge every evening and leaning on the railing. Instead of looking towards Jacque's office, I would look here and there. The unease of this separation had shrunk into a pit and settled in the midst of my heartbeats, which I leapt over without noticing. My attention kept wandering to below the bridge. He was always sitting there. For many days I watched him sitting on the bench and reading. There was a strange attraction in the way he sat and read his book but more so in his total, unwavering concentration. Invariably, my gaze was drawn to him. Then one evening, I took a long, circuitous detour, went down the bridge and sat on the other corner of the bench.

He didn't look up from his book. Wanting to talk to him, I kept sitting there. A faint darkness began settling down on the edge of the river. It soon thickened. The bench too was shrouded in darkness and the lights on the bridge started flickering. Their reflection turned the river into a glittering sheet. Slowly he looked up from his book and gazed at the flowing river; it seemed like he was sitting, not on a public bench, but in his own room, peeping out of the window. After a few minutes, he turned towards me hesitantly, perhaps afraid that he was invading my privacy. Then he looked ahead again, groped for his books lying next to him, gathered them and started to get up.

'Do you come here every day to read?'

He looked at me in some surprise. For the first time, I felt that he had registered my presence.

'The library lends books for only two weeks,' he said as if he was half awake, half asleep. Books clasped in his hands, he stood up quickly. In his hurry, one of the books fell. Before he could retrieve it, I picked it up and began turning its pages as I fell into step with him. It was a book of letters shared between some Rilke and Marina Tsvetaeva. I tried to read a bit but found it difficult. I only managed a few words, and the story behind them was quite lost on me. I looked at him from the corner of my eye to check whether he had seen me turning the pages. He was walking straight ahead.

He was doing research in philosophy at the Sorbonne.

'Will you teach philosophy?' I once asked him. He was sitting on the same bench.

'I want to do something else,' he replied very softly. There was humility in his voice, but there was even more resolve and determination. I kept looking at him. I had never encountered such delicate determination before.

'We go to literature and philosophy to look for and to open the paths to understanding ourselves and the world. Philosophy illuminates these paths, but the role of literature is unique. After giving us a brief glimpse of finding ourselves, it keeps alive that desire, always, perennially. Perhaps music, theatre, cinema also do this ...'

The words coming out of his mouth seemed to sparkle and shine. I didn't understand much, but the luminosity of his words lit up my innermost being for a moment or two. He would look into my eyes when he would start talking, then he would first take his gaze to the corner of my eyes and from there shift it far away, as if he was gently pulling out my vision and expanding it far beyond.

He never once asked me how long I had been looking at him sitting on the bench, or why. He never asked me why I suddenly became sad while talking to him. His curiosity lay in different directions. For instance, he was very interested in knowing how well I understood French and whether I had read French poets in their original language. Who did I like among them? As if he was trying to find out about me from a distance, the distance afforded by books and poetry. Or maybe he was concerned with only that much of my being that floated between us and didn't want to bother with the rest. Despite this, I always felt that it was he alone who understood me well and shared each one of my sorrows without saying a word, as if he could sense every painful tremor of my life from behind the veil of books and literature. The distance between us wasn't lonely or empty; the heartbeats of our intimacy began to slowly fill that void. However, distance was necessary for this intimacy, and that is where the heartbeats that kept our relationship alive reverberated. It was difficult to close that gap, nor did I want to. I found myself expanding in the space between us and that was the space where my memories took on a new shape. We would go to art galleries together and look at the paintings for hours.

From ancient Egyptian reliefs to Cezanne's paintings of Mont Sainte-Victoire, from Rodin's sculptures to Picasso's paintings and paper works, we saw it all, after which we would sit in the restaurants outside the museums and galleries for hours and share our experiences, sometimes with silences, sometimes with words. If, in the solitude of a park, I sometimes tried to touch him, he wouldn't refuse, but I would feel as if he was standing a little behind the lips I was touching, looking at the two of us and smiling.

I couldn't stop him. How could I have stopped him? Our warmth and closeness lived in the distance between us. I didn't have the courage to wipe that out. He went away, and the distance between us increased so much that our togetherness was reduced to just a sensation for both of us. I was with him in India, he was with me in Paris, and we were alone in both places.

A villager saw the crowd in the courtyard, and he too went inside. He stayed in a village temple and sometimes came to town to wander around a little. From that day on, the day when he would come to town was fixed.

Lakhna

It was all memsaab's goodness of heart, otherwise the police spared no effort to trap Lakhna. It was memsaab who stepped in and had Lakhanlal freed. Otherwise, he would have been beaten so much that all his bones would have been broken. How long does it take to proclaim a poor person a thief or a murderer? They thrash you till you confess. You have no choice but to say, 'Yes, our lord and master, we are the thieves … yes, we are the murderers.' You have to say what they want to hear. They dragged me to the police station heedlessly, without pausing to think for even a second. I kept saying, 'Saab, I haven't done anything, I was sleeping outside. How do I know what happened, how it happened …' But no, they didn't listen to a word. Why would they? I was saying what they didn't want to hear. I should have said what they did want to hear. Then they would have listened. I kept saying, 'Saab, I haven't done anything …' But the inspector kept hitting me, went on with the thrashing. How much he cursed and abused. Each abuse worse than the one hurled before it. The abuses didn't spare anyone in my family. This is the problem with being poor and penniless in this country: no one is willing to believe you. You doubt yourself all the time, how will someone else believe you? I kept pleading innocence, he kept on beating me. When he got tired, he gave his baton to someone else. They thought they would get me to vomit out the words they wanted to hear.

'After being hammered so much, the bastard will spit out what we want to hear.'

I kept getting beaten. But how could I say something I didn't know anything about. So, nothing came out of my mouth, and blue streaks silently appeared on my body. Who knows where these blue streaks were hidden in Lakhanlal's body that they came out with the police beating, rippling and swelling. Even today, those wavy blue streaks continue to ripple down my back, like crawling snakes. It's as if I feel the pain from the beating move through them – from right to left and left to right. Had I come here from Lumbini for this? I have a farm back home. A five-year-old daughter. Saheb was always worried about her. He told me repeatedly that I must educate her! But where were the good schools back home where I could educate her? I am happy just seeing Noa bibi. It's enough that my old parents are looking after my wife and children. How can I ask them to educate my child as well? That they feed her, take care of her with so much love – is this not enough of a burden on my chest? But who could explain all this to saheb. He's like a saint; he thinks everyone is like him.

Lakhna told him so many times that saheb, these uncles of Vandana memsaab are no good, that they go around abusing him, but he always laughed it off. 'Lakhna, I deserve to be abused. Poor things, if they don't abuse me, what will they do, worship me?' How could anyone kill a man like him? Someone said this is all Vandana's uncles' doing. It could be. But the police need evidence, and they only know one way to gather it: beat someone up. Even illiterate people like me find the police uncivilised and barbarous. Why don't you go and catch Kishore Lal Kothari kesarwale? He roamed around abusing saheb, but no one said anything to him – instead they caught me; me, who had never uttered a word against him. They caught me. Me, for whom saheb was the sole support.

I can't even leave memsaab and Noa bibi now, otherwise Lakhanlal would have run away long ago. Saheb has died, but he isn't gone. He will be watching, from somewhere, what everyone is up to. I too must go there one day, and then saheb will ask me, Lakhna, you left Noa bibi and memsaab and ran away. Will I not have to hang my head in shame then? Saheb will ask about Vandana memsaab also. Lakhna will tell him that saheb, after your death, all the light went out of her; she died inside long ago. The body that you see now, that's nothing more than her shadow. When she phones, her voice trembles so much, I am afraid she might stumble and fall, still holding the receiver. She asks after Noa bibi, and as God is my witness, she is also worried about Mridula memsaab. Once I broke down on the phone and wept. Vandana memsaab said, 'Lakhna, you must control yourself. If Noa bibi sees you like this, what will she think?'

Memsaab, Noa bibi asks me such questions about Baba day and night, I feel like smashing my head somewhere. How can I answer her questions? She is so intelligent, saheb's darling child, she has a mind just like saheb's.

Even today, I am saheb's servant. The police can say what it wants. I have always slept in the outside verandah. Saheb never said anything; if I wanted, I could have slept in the living room – I do anyway in the winter – but I like the verandah. It's as if I am lying in a flying machine. That's where I was sitting, waiting to be scolded. I'd got late fetching Noa bibi. This was saheb's one weakness – he was scared for Noa bibi. I don't know what his fear was. I don't know if he confided in anyone about it. He never said anything to me. Why would he say anything to me? I am hardly the cleverest person around. How can Lakhanlal assuage someone else's fear. He is himself a scared person. Saheb had a strange way of doing things. He would scold me to his heart's content, and then, when he would feel he had gone too far, he would immediately laugh and say, 'Lakhna, tell me, why do you refer to yourself as Lakhanlal instead of "I"?'

I often wondered what this man was made of. There was a kernel of laughter hidden even in his anger. I nicked five–ten rupees from his pocket dozens of times. Maybe he never figured it out, but even if he did, he never asked me about it. I would often feel ashamed of myself, that I was cheating a man who was not even aware he was being cheated, but one is often faced with scarcity. So I would take the money with the understanding that it was a loan taken from saheb without his knowledge, and I would repay it whenever I could.

If you were late taking tea for saheb, no scolding. His clothes were not ironed, no scolding. He would do it himself without saying a word. If saheb came home late at night and you took time to open the door, no scolding. Sometimes you took a swig or two and lay down and the verandah started smelling, no scolding. Even when you were late delivering his food to the library, he would just say, 'Okay,' without looking up, put it on the table and not say another word. But if you were a little late picking up Noa bibi, he would let you have it. A solid scolding. So that night I was bound to get it. And I did. A solid scolding.

'Lakhna, why are you such an idiot. I have told you a thousand times, even if you are dying, you can't be late in picking up Noa. How did you get late? You must have stopped somewhere to chew tobacco. There is no hope for you, you are made this way; you can't help but be careless. For one, you picked her up late, and then you immediately went to sleep as well. You didn't have the sense to realise that she is alone, the little girl is alone, she will get scared. Let her get scared, it's more important for us to sleep. Why didn't you phone me? Why don't you say something?'

When saheb began his scolding, he wouldn't stop. He wouldn't listen to anyone or anything in the middle. When he got tired and calmed down, Lakhanlal got his chance.

'Actually, saheb, I went to drop memsaab to the hospital. She was burning with fever. She was worried she might collapse in the three-wheeler even before reaching the hospital. There was some time before I had to pick up Noa bibi, so I thought I would drop memsaab to the hospital and then go to the maidan. That's how Lakhanlal got a bit late.'

'All right,' saheb said and began walking to his room. Then he must have felt that he had scolded me a little too much. He promptly turned around and, with the same angry face, said, 'But why do you refer to yourself as 'Lakhanlal' instead of "I"?'

This was the last time Lakhanlal saw saheb alive. He picked up Noa bibi and carried her to his room. I came out to the verandah and lay down. I was anyway drowsy, and I hadn't been scolded enough to banish my sleepiness. I kept sleeping. What happened to saheb that night, and when, I had no clue. Look at my fate; the support of my life was being snatched away from me just a few steps away, and I was grandly sleeping away on the floor. The police were right to beat up Lakhanlal. He deserved it. Inside, saheb was going through so much pain, and here was Lakhanlal, deaf to everything. And now I am flinching at Noa bibi's questions. Oh

God! What can I say to this little girl, where has her Baba gone. Has anyone ever got to know? Once Kishan maharaj crossed the Yamuna, he didn't turn back. The gopis were exhausted from weeping; saheb is, after all, a human being. Once you have gone across, how can you come back?

The police can ask whatever it wants. The inspector kept beating me with his baton, asking, 'What was your saheb's relationship with Vandana? Talk! She used to come to your saheb's house, no? What did the two of them do? Tell me!'

Weeping, I would say, 'Don't slander a dead man, inspector saheb! How do I know what their relationship was? You can beat me all you want, but I can only tell you what I know.'

'Stop talking rubbish. When your skin comes off your buttocks, all this arrogance will vanish.'

My eyes welled up when his baton struck me. Lakhanlal didn't know that all the tears that remained unshed at saheb's passing – because he was scared for Noa bibi – all those suppressed tears were destined to come out from the beating by the police. From their batons. Otherwise, does it look nice to cry at such a ripe age as mine. Now how will I face saheb there. I had thought I would tie up my tears in a bundle and take it up there and tell saheb, 'See, saheb, I may refer to myself as Lakhanlal, but this bundle was never opened in front of Noa bibi. I brought it all tied up, just like it was.'

But who was there to listen to me. The inspector was growling like a crazy dog.

'Whenever I saw saheb and Vandana memsaab together, they were always reading. Saheb would be reading to her from an open book or Vandana memsaab would be reading to him. Once or twice, I also saw them deep in conversation.'

'What kind of conversation?'

'How could I make that out? Lakhanlal couldn't even follow saheb's ordinary conversation, any kind of deep talk was out of the question. All I can tell you is that it seemed as if some rishi-munis were conversing at Naimisharanya. How do I know what they were talking about? If I understood that, wouldn't I have also lapped up the Bhavsagar, the sea of existence. Would I be here at the police station? You should have seen their faces when they were together, inspector saheb. They would glow, as if lit up by the rising sun. Many times, Noa bibi would come and sit on Vandana memsaab's lap. Saheb would stop mid-sentence and go into the kitchen to make tea while Vandana memsaab kept chatting to Noa bibi. She adored her.'

'Adore her, indeed. Your saheb has driven her crazy. Understood, saheb's pimp!'

'How can that be, inspector saheb. How can someone who shows you the light drive you mad. It doesn't matter what we think or say. I know that Vandana memsaab and saheb showed each other the light. Light. That is why their faces glowed. Glimmered. Shimmered.'

A beautiful woman, with long hair swinging below her waist, would arrive right at the end. But in a few years' time, she became the first to arrive. Her eyes reflected a mix of eagerness and sadness.

Saanvli

No. Nobody called for me. I have come just like that. Your book had no place for me, but here I am. I couldn't help it. Thought that I should stay here for a while. No, it is not because I want to get rid of any tiredness; I just want to offload my story. Yes, I will tell you. Yes, I am the same girl, Vandana's tau's daughter – the same one who studied and worked, because of which he had to keep answering thousands of questions, all kinds of questions. Vandana didn't reveal my name. Maybe she thought of it but didn't let it out. I will tell you. Saanvli is my name. First, it was Saanvri, but when my father got me admitted to school, the teacher corrected it to Saanvli. Meaning, the first part of my name was given by my father, the second by my teacher. In this scuffle between these two parts, my life was over. Don't be startled. What I have just said is the truth. My life was finished. Meaning, it was spent, exhausted. Meaning, it was over. All of it. After it was spent, it was thrown away into an empty room. Because the others didn't understand what I was saying, and I didn't understand what they were saying. But this happens to everyone. Has anyone ever understood what anyone else is saying? I know no one has; they just pretend they have. The one who is explaining everything is reassured by this. The listener is also satisfied that once again he hasn't failed in pretending that he has understood the other.

Neither my son nor my daughter comes to talk to me in that empty room. The husband is anyway an embodiment of God and God's natural quality is that He stays out of reach. There was enough light in the room. There was a window too on one of the walls. Behind the window was the sky, spread out over millions of miles; you could see birds in the sky every morning and evening. But I got tired. Tired of doing nothing. This tiredness of doing nothing is very different from the tiredness that comes from doing things. You can dispel the tiredness that comes from doing things by lazing around. But the tiredness that comes from doing nothing never goes away; it keeps accumulating, not in your body, not in your mind, but somewhere else, that is a part of you, but you don't have a word for it in your language. Or maybe I just don't know it. There must be a word for it. You people are experts at creating words for each and every thing. When you have even found a word for not living, then what's the big deal about anything else? As soon as a problematic situation arises, you quickly place a word on it like a lid. You have found a great way to bring problematic situations and inexplicable things under your control: give them a name. But you don't really give it a name, you only cover it with a lid. Every single thing that is beyond your understanding.

I was tired. Perhaps this happened because I had been called by a strange name. Who knows? In the beginning, someone or the other used to come to my room and would even try to talk to me. My mother would cajole me, 'Be patient, girl, be patient!' My father would also come. He would look at me and go away. My son and daughter were kept away from me. Perhaps they didn't want to come to see me. Who knows. My husband, my lord and master, was busy with his work. It was enough for him that I was there, somewhere.

But *he* didn't come. He could have just come and stood somewhere far away in the millions of miles of sky spread out outside the window. For a couple of seconds. I would have had my fill of looking at him, then he could have gone.

But he wasn't going to come, and so he didn't appear anywhere near the window. My eyes turned lifeless, but he didn't melt. Oh, I forgot to mention that I have died, staying in that closed room, day after day. Meaning, I have become that to which all of you have given a name, which all of you call dead. Don't be shocked as to how a dead girl is going on talking. (Oh God, I am still referring to myself as 'girl'. Just look at me, I have never been able to think of myself as a 'woman'!) What of it? Alive or dead, everyone speaks. People who write don't make a distinction between the two. It is not as if the one who writes only listens to those who are alive and tells the dead to keep quiet. Poor thing, he doesn't know how to do this. He listens to everybody. You too listen to everybody. Never mind who is dead and who is not. No, I won't be able to tell you about that. I can't tell you what happens after you die, etc. That can't be explained in your intelligent language. And anyway, why should I say all that, things you won't even be able to pretend you understand. And it is nothing very special anyway. And you are not going to be around forever. Once you leave, you'll see everything on this side for yourself.

I was sure he would come. He wouldn't be able to take me out of the room (not that I wanted to go). But I was sure that he would definitely come. Definitely. With my ear to the door, I would listen intently to people's conversations, in case someone brought up his name by mistake, then I would get to know where he was, how he was, what he was doing. Not so I could go there. Who would let me go out. But because then I could imagine what he was doing. Where he would be. I needed just a little information about him to think of him in my imagination. I didn't even get that. Sitting on the floor, I would listen to what was being said outside with great attention. They would talk of everything except him. The moment I felt the conversation might turn to him, I would try to listen even more carefully, I would be totally absorbed in it, but the people talking were so clever, they would change the topic before his name could come up.

I would be left as desolate as ever. If I had just one brick of information about him, I would have built an entire mansion in my imagination, but I wasn't destined to get even that one brick.

Often, I would feel a sharp pull in my veins, as if every fibre of my body, not just my mind, was agitating to be with him, was desperate to be with him. I would roll about on the floor. If someone came into the room just then to give me food, they would scream, 'Oh, the girl is getting fits!' Did you hear that – this is your language, your intelligent language, where 'longing' is called a fit. In the time it would take everyone in the house to gather and for some of them to start their hocus-pocus exorcism tricks, I, lying on the floor, would sense this fever of longing slowly abating.

He had come close to me by not being there.

'The fever of longing!' Wah, what a beautiful phrase. I have no quarrel with this one. It has stood by me, been my companion. I have passed the difficult days of my life with its comforting presence. I may not get another chance in your book, so, burning and getting snuffed out in this phrase, let me quickly see a few scenes out of so many, just one more time. Yes, one more time. I am going to school in these scenes. To college. My fragrant days, my flower days.

I had to cross a nearby village on the way, and Ma would say every day, 'Why is Saanvri going to school?' Every day my father would explain to her, 'There is no literate girl apart from her in the village.' Two plaits, two red ribbons. Ma would sit on the ground and make me sit in front of her, between her feet, and she would plait my hair with such force, it was like she wanted to tie me up. My plaits were so tight that the ends would curl up. Instead of dangling down, the ribbons would stay upright. Like two red roses in bloom. I would hop, skip and jump my way to school, bouncing about like a ball. As if I was going to another world. Anyone I met on the way wouldn't forget to remark:

'The girl is going to school.'

It wasn't a long way off. Splashes of sunshine fell gently, spreading over the morning dew dotting the ground, as if to take the dew back to the sky. The mist of the night, hovering over the small pond like a sheet, would try to see its reflection in the water before vanishing. I would walk on the side of the road for a while, then go through the fields. Imprints of the sun would be scattered over the mustard fields. I would hop on the ridges in the fields and reach school. Some fields had rows of guava trees. The mango trees were planted in such a way that they looked like elderly people standing in a semi-circle, holding hands on a hot afternoon. I don't know how, but there were plenty of jackfruit trees with bunches of jackfruits hanging all over. They looked like they were about to fall off. I would go back home from school, skirting these trees, throwing stones at the guavas, splashing about in the pond for a while.

Once home, I would spread my textbooks and notebooks all over the courtyard. Everyone would say:

'The girl studies a lot!'

For me, school was a dream as much as it was a place to study. As if it was a world apart from my world. I really did study a lot. My teacher was very fond of me. That slim teacher always told me:

'Saanvli, you must study a lot. A lot. There is no point if a girl studies a little and then stops halfway through. If you end up doing that, your family will reproach you.'

I would study all night during the exams and top the class. I leapt from one class to the next. Apart from me, there were two other girls in the school. Both hopeless at studies. I didn't feel like talking to the boys. The only person I spoke to was Teacher. There were other teachers too, men and women, but there was only one I spoke to freely. She was the one I called Teacher. She always kept me by her side. She wanted to keep me with her even after classes got over. Even during break time, I would be with her. She would make all kinds of savoury fried treats for me. Her colleagues would tease her:

'Why don't you adopt Saanvli?'

Teacher would smile and not say anything.

One day, she got transferred to a school in a neighbouring village. She had to leave our school. At first, I didn't understand what was going on, but slowly it sank in that she had gone and wouldn't come back. I cried for months. Ma and my father were vexed. Going to school became a burden for me. After setting off from home, the moment I realised Teacher wouldn't be there, I would go back home. And then I wouldn't move from there. I would lie in bed all day. I would glance at my textbooks, notebooks and satchel and burst into tears. The textbooks, notebooks, satchels, the walls of the room would first blur, then start sinking before my tear-filled eyes.

At his wits' end, one day, my father went and brought Teacher home. As soon as I saw her, I sobbed my heart out. She too kept crying. After some time, she tried to explain things to me. I didn't understand anything but drank in her words like a man thirsty for water. As if the roots of a dried-up plant, deprived of water for weeks, were suddenly surrounded by moisture and dampness. It was as though life began speeding up my every vein. I sensed repeated echoes of my own being from every fibre of my body. She took me in her lap and said she would come once a week to see me at school.

She left, and immediately my satchel was packed. Every day, I waited for her more than

I studied in school. The whole day would pass, and she wouldn't come. But there would always be that one day when I didn't wait in vain. She would come during break time and take me outside the school to sit under the shade of a dense tamarind tree. I would lie down with my head in her lap, and she would stroke my hair and talk to me softly. I never remembered what she said, but her love for me dripped from every word she uttered. When the shade of the tamarind tree would slip away from above us and recede into the distance, Teacher would tell me to go back to school, and picking up her bag, she would return to her own school. I would stand below the tamarind tree for a long time, watching her disappear gradually.

The days she wouldn't come, I would stop by in some field on my way home, put my satchel below a mango or guava tree, take off my chunri, spread it on the satchel and lie down with my head on it, pretending I was lying in Teacher's lap. I would lie down like this for some time, then get up and go home. One day, when I was lying like this in Teacher's make-believe lap, I felt Teacher bending and kissing my forehead. Eyes closed, I continued lying down. Then I felt Teacher cup my face in her hands and kiss my eyes. She's caressing me so lovingly today, I thought and could no longer keep my eyes closed. But there was no Teacher anywhere there. Nobody was there. The leaves of the nearby trees stirred softly in the air. I got up with a fright. I put my dupatta back on my shoulders, grabbed my satchel and ran home. By the time I reached home, the touch that my body had soaked in thinking it was Teacher's began floating to the surface again. I felt as if scores of ants were crawling on my eyes and forehead. I kept trying to brush them away with my hands when I reached home. As soon as she saw me, Ma said, 'What happened to you, girl, why is your face so red?'

'Red, how do you mean red?'

I was already agitated by those strange ants. Now this redness of my face!

'As if you had blushed deeply,' she said and laughed loudly.

'Are you crazy? On whose account would I feel so abashed? Why should I feel shy?' I said, irritated.

Ma controlled herself, but she couldn't get rid of the smile on her face. She went away.

Teacher came the next day. Once again, we sat in the shade of the tamarind tree. I told her about yesterday afternoon's incident. Except about the ants. Or I would have had to tell her about Ma laughing at me too. She was lost in thought for a little while, then, eyes full of tears, she said haltingly, 'It's not good to love so much, Saanvli!'

As always, I only heard the tone of her voice, the way she spoke; I hardly ever heard the words she spoke anyway.

The next afternoon, I didn't stop at the field on the way back, I almost ran past it. It wasn't exactly fear; it was a kind of dark frisson that blazed through my body like lightning when I thought of that day. But after a few days there was a curiosity, an eagerness to stop and see what would happen. Returning from school, I put down my satchel below the guava tree, spread my chunri over it and lay down on the grass with my eyes closed. I heard the voice of a farmer in the nearby field for a long time. He was singing something. Then that voice quieted down. I felt someone removing my shoes. Nervous and a little panicky, I continued lying down quietly. Now I felt the touch of someone's hand on my foot, then the pressure of someone's lips on my right sole. I hurriedly got up. Rattled, he fell backwards with a thud. As he got up, ready to flee, I grabbed his hand.

'What were you doing?' I snapped.

'Touching your feet!'

'Why?'

'I thought a fairy had descended, wearing a villager's clothes!'

'So?'

'I have heard that if you touch a fairy with your lips, you will get married to her!'

He was a fair, sturdily built boy. Dishevelled golden hair fell on his forehead. Eyes as innocent and guileless as the lake below. He was wearing a shirt and, below it, a dhoti. I wanted to burst out laughing, but I controlled myself. Assuming a severe expression, I said, 'And if despite this the fairy doesn't want to marry you, then what?'

'The fairy has no wish of her own; her wishes are the wishes of anyone who brings her under his control!'

At this, I could no longer control myself. Instead of being angry, I started laughing. At first, he seemed nervous. For him fairies were probably meant for marriage, they weren't supposed to laugh. But in no time, his face brightened. He too started laughing. Still laughing, he came a little closer to me. Quietly, he took my plait in his hand and just as quietly kissed the ribbon. I understood that he was still trying to bring the fairy under his control. I said nothing. Suddenly he stood up and yelled, 'Oh, I am dead!'

He promptly sped away. I stayed for a long time, listening to the sound of his running feet. As soon as the sound died out, I felt all the blood in my body rush to my face.

'Was this what Ma called feeling shy?'

Teacher didn't come the next day. As was my habit, I went and lay down beneath the guava tree. God knows where he came from, silent-footed, and kissed my open palm, which was lying on the grass, facing the sky. I went numb. He got up, went to the other side, tenderly lifted my other hand in both his hands, bent his head, opened my palm and placed his lips on it. I closed my palm. His nose got caught in my fist. He screamed so loudly that I shrank back. I let go of his nose.

'What happened?' I asked.

'Who knows what a fairy may do; she may kill you.'

I started laughing. I laughed so much, my eyes closed of their own volition. When they opened, I saw him standing there, holding a handful of flowers.

'Where did you get these?'

'They fell from the fairy's mouth when she was laughing. I collected them.'

He kept touching me, and the fairy kept falling deeper and deeper under his control.

He started dropping his fairy to school. The fairy's school finished, she went to the city to study in college. He would come there every week. We would go together to the park. Sitting there, he would tell me all kinds of stories. He would often ask me about the stories I was being taught in college. I would answer, 'None.' He would be astonished. He couldn't understand why I went to college if I was not being told any stories there. I don't know which world he belonged to. He would spend all his time telling stories. Those stories were his home. His courtyard. His own country, a foreign country. He would place every event in his life inside a story to understand it. 'This is just like what happened once upon a time …'

This was the 'fever of longing' that held me in thrall for so many years. Look what it did to me. It could do the same to anyone. There is no knowing who it would choose as its fairy. It was my good fortune that this time I was chosen as the fairy. A fairy, who had no wish of her own; her wishes became those of the one who had her under his control. I won't tell you anything more. There is nothing more to tell anyway. But before leaving, I will say it one more time: 'fever of longing'.

There were six steps after the courtyard. The stairs were littered with neem leaves from the nearby tree. Patches of faded light from the setting sun were trapped in one corner. The fruit of the neem tree looked like the fruit of the sun.

Thief

I shouldn't have brought a weapon with me. But I always carried one and nothing had ever happened before.

This happened for the first time.

I don't know how it happened.

The last twitch of that good man's hand before it stilled forever has been hammered into my forehead like a nail. I had no intention of doing anything like that, and why would I. I am an ordinary thief; I had gone there for a bit of petty thieving. Now I don't even remember exactly what happened, or why I did what I did. How did it happen, how? I did try to stop it, but in that fog of fear, by the time I could stop myself, the damage had already been done.

I rushed out of the house, washed my hands at the garden tap and ran out, panting, to the footpath. A row of beggars was sleeping there. I lay down in their midst. But do hands really get cleaned like this? How did I do something like this? If I hadn't had the weapon in my hands, this wouldn't have happened. At the most, he would have handed me over to the police, I would have stayed in jail for a few days, then left. But now I am in the grip of something – I don't know what – and I can't seem to get out of it, no matter how much I try. Now what is the point of thinking what if I didn't have the weapon in my hands. Once something has happened, it cannot be undone, no matter how much you want it. It gets stuck in your mind forever – you can hide it, cover it, but you can't remove it. I keep going off to sleep, hoping that at some point I will wake up and find that none of it is true, that it took place in a dream. But that never happens. Instead, all through the dream, I am aware of what I have done outside the dream, and the dream is where I have come to hide.

It has been so many days since I have worked. I can't bring myself to go. I feel someone will see the blood dripping from my hands. I can hear his suppressed groan of pain from behind my back. How many times, how many times I have heard it. It sounds stifled each time I hear it. As if he wasn't letting himself groan loudly. My knife is buried in the left side of his stomach, and he is trying, quietly, slowly, to pull it out while staring at me, his eyes stretched wide open. He looks like he is about to scream, but it is as if someone has stopped the scream in his throat with their hands.

Why was he trying to stop this, his last scream? Why, why, why? So that the neighbours wouldn't wake up, and I wouldn't get caught? No, how can that be? Why wouldn't he want me to get caught? I had come to his house to steal, and it was my hands that had held the knife now buried in his stomach. That he was trying to save me, no, this wasn't possible. Not at all. Then why didn't he scream? Was it because he didn't know how to scream? That's not possible either. The sound that came from his throat was a stifled scream; it was as if the moment that scream was released, someone had swiftly snuffed it out. Poured water over it. He could have screamed; his face showed that he could have screamed with full force. But he didn't. Why, why, why? Was he not in the habit of screaming? But who has a habit of screaming except a policeman? Does anyone scream out of habit? Nor was there an overwhelming fear in his eyes that I could say he didn't scream because he was too frightened. There was no fear on his face, only a kind of innocence, as if he saw something strange on my face. No, no, it wasn't fear. There was some other reason behind his not screaming.

There it is. I have come back, scared, to that very place. To that place I never wanted to return to again. The place I have been struggling to run away from. He didn't scream because …

because his little girl was sound asleep in his bed. He didn't scream till his dying breath because that little slip of a girl might wake up. What kind of man did I murder? What kind of man was this, holding on to his last scream so that his sleeping child wouldn't wake up in the middle of the night. And his eyes, I can still see what I saw in his eyes. As if he was saying that sentence which keeps sinking deeper and deeper into every part of my body like so many nails: Why did you kill me, bhai? There was no anger in his eyes nor was there the contempt one is used to seeing in most people's eyes. No, there was none of that. There was only a mild reproach. Will anyone believe that there was just this mild reproach in those drowning eyes, as if I hadn't knifed him in the stomach but just dropped some ink on his trousers, and he had exclaimed: Why have you dropped this ink, bhai? Why don't you look where you are going?

I was left standing frozen in front of him. As if I had forgotten how to walk. Because I had panicked and inadvertently used my knife, he was dying before my eyes, and I couldn't do anything about it. My feet were rooted to the ground. I wanted to run to him and pull the knife out. But I just couldn't do it. I wanted to flee as fast as I could from this circle of death in front of me. But my feet had turned to lead, and I couldn't lift them. Like someone had tied stones to them. My eyes could not look away as he slowly fell to the floor. As if someone had bored my gaze into his death. He had stopped looking at me. One hand was trying to hold on to the bed, the other was flailing in the air. When he finally fell to the floor, he somehow managed to rest his face on the bed. Both his trembling hands slowly inched towards the little girl sleeping on the bed. I got frightened that the moment his hands touched her, she would wake up. I turned and tried to run. But my feet were still not my own. They were made of lead. His hands became still before they could reach the little girl, and in the middle of that cold night, his head rolled over to one side, on the corner of the bed.

He was gone.

I sleepwalked my way out of the house. The bright light from the street lamps could not pierce the thick fog to reach the ground. You could vaguely make out the street only because of the row of pale lights. Nothing was moving, as if I had stuck my knife not only into him, but into the very body of the night. Into the whole world. The servant of the house was sleeping in the verandah, covered by a blanket. I hadn't come out the way I had gone inside. Then, the thought that I might get caught hadn't even entered my mind. Like his blood, my mind was also frozen. I opened the door and came out into the verandah. In the darkness, the shape of the sleeping servant looked even darker. Once I came out of the house, I regained a little of my consciousness. I ran to the corner of the garden and washed my hands under a running tap. In that cold, running water, the dried, jammed blood on my hands started leaching out.

A small crowd is gathered in the verandah. Some people are standing in front of the table, a few have formed little groups and are chatting to each other, holding their teacups. On the other side of the table, a thin young man is smiling and pouring tea into the cups.

Kishore

Now why am I wandering around, complaining to everyone. I was the one who had called him over. I was the one who had gone to the library fully prepared, and I was the one who had composed a beautiful sentence in my head to invite him home, never mind that I ended up saying something else instead. I was so eager to have him come home. I had decided to shut the shop in the afternoon itself. He was to come in the evening. I wanted to get home by the afternoon. I was feeling a little sheepish about this uncalled-for enthusiasm. I started telling myself, who is this Sudipt babu after all, about whose visit you are so excited. You want to shut shop and go home? A small-time librarian and you are behaving as if a sadhu or mahatma is coming to grace your house. Don't you remember how he had asked you so sarcastically, 'You will give me saffron-laced milk, won't you?' He was reminding you of your trade, and you are unnecessarily working yourself up about him. First see to your business, then shut your shop at leisure and go home. Even if he comes, he can wait for a while. Thinking all this, I didn't go home despite wanting to. Should I go or should I not go – I was trapped by my indecision. As daylight started waning, a lot of customers landed up at the shop all at once. I had a thought at the back of my mind that there was a festival that day. Many people come to buy saffron on festival days. I found it quite natural that so many customers had turned up at the shop. I caught myself saying a few times, 'After all, it's a festival …' Suddenly the shop attendant Ramswarup said, 'Babu ji, what festival is it today? There are no festivals these days nor in the days to come. These are plain, empty, dry days.'

'Plain, empty, dry days!' Startled, I kept staring at him. That is when I knew that no matter how hard I tried to convince myself otherwise, deep inside, I did think of his coming home as a special occasion. This eagerness arose from inside me, from some deep recesses I had no control over. Without wanting to, I felt a soft wave of happiness course through me. I was helpless before this unwanted joy. I handed over the keys to Ramswarup and began putting on my shoes. Ramswarup could only gape at me. This was the first time I was giving him the responsibility of closing the shop. I felt ashamed at his surprise and a little sad that I had never trusted him enough till today.

Caught in this pull and push between shame and sadness, I huffed and puffed my way home, only to find that Sudipt was already there. I heard his voice from outside the door. At that point I did not realise in the slightest that the clouds of our problems had already begun gathering over us. We couldn't see that which had started unfolding in front of our eyes at exactly that moment. Sudipt was sitting in the drawing room. Vandana, holding a tray, was standing at the door that led inside the house. Seeing them I felt relieved that Bhabhi had asked Vandana to ensure Sudipt was seated comfortably in my absence. He didn't see me for a few moments, even after I entered the room; me, who had been waiting for him the whole day. I didn't feel bad. But I did find it strange. How could a person sitting in my own house show such disdain for me? Vandana too didn't seem to recognise me. But I didn't think this way for too long. The thought had floated up to me, and just like that, it floated away. They were talking about books. He was deep in conversation, telling Vandana to read a particular book. This was his way. He was unrivalled in the art of getting the other person totally engrossed in conversation. That day, I too was awed by this ability of his. Such was the absorption that the world silently dissolved around us, only his voice remained – soft, level, rhythmic. The tray was shaking in Vandana's hand. Staring fixedly at the floor, Vandana wasn't so much listening to his voice as she was drinking it in, like someone who has been thirsty for a long time. That is why, for a few moments, she didn't notice that I had come in. They kept talking, and I wondered if I was made of glass or air.

When this began happening time and again, sometimes at home, sometimes in the library, where he had cleverly started inviting Vandana, I had an intuitive feeling about what was going on. I became alert; something was brewing between the two of them. Leaving the shop to Ramswarup, I would suddenly land up in the library on winter afternoons. Vandana would often be there. She always looked happy. Sometimes she would be reading alone. Sometimes she would be with Sudipt. Often, she would be talking to Alim. I would cough loudly in the library, sometimes deliberately drop a book so that Vandana would notice that I had caught her talking to men who were outsiders. There wasn't the slightest awareness on her face that she had been caught. Instead, she would look at me as if she hadn't seen me. As though she wasn't looking at her uncle but a stranger. I would go down the stairs, muttering under my breath.

On that first day there was not a trace of resentment or bitterness in me. I listened quietly to them talking. It was getting dark outside, and the light from the bulb was getting brighter inside. The sound of the wind rustling through the tall trees outside wafted all over. Birds had flown in from somewhere, then flown far away somewhere else. I peered out of the window. The cars in the street had switched on their headlights. The roar of passing motorcycles would suddenly fill the room, and Sudipt and Vandana's words would get lost in the sound. Meanwhile, Bhabhi had already called out twice to Vandana. But Vandana's feet remained stuck at the door. The tray was shaking in her hands. Her long black plait swung down her back.

Not more than two or three minutes had passed. But I felt as if it had been a long time. Oh! All that talk. That is why I must have felt that time had slowed down. The conversation that took place before me that evening went on and on. It went on for so long that it spread over days, weeks, months and years, in the verandahs and rooms of his library, in who knows how many parks and corners of the city. Silently, I kept looking at him talking. Vandana suddenly turned and disappeared behind the curtain. For a couple of seconds, we sat with our heads bent, without saying a word to each other. Then Sudipt looked at me and spoke, his voice sounding as if it was coming from far away. 'Kishore, can I smoke here?'

There was not the slightest trace of guilt on his face at having taken no notice of me all this while. On the contrary, his face reflected a deep serenity. I could only stare at his brazenness. Before I could say anything, he took the cigarettes and matchbox out of his pocket. One side of the collar of his check shirt was twisted oddly, maybe the second or third button was undone. The tip of a handkerchief was peeping out of the pocket of his blue jeans. I kept looking at it for a while without thinking of anything in particular. My enthusiasm towards him had cooled. My dislike for him had slowly started spreading its wings. I realised that I would come to hate him in the coming days.

Often a sharp gust of wind would blow over the stairs and all the way inside, rumpling the light brown tablecloth covering the tea table. You could see the gleaming wood of the table in the verandah lights.

Alim

I don't think I can accept abba's advice to improve my prospects now. It is true that I did not want to remain stuck in the library forever. I wanted to leave. I did not see much of a future here. Time and again, I found myself agreeing with abba.

'You will rot in this library, miyan. Use your time there to study and learn, then sit for some big competitive exam and get a proper job.'

This rundown building; its hundred-and-fifty-year-old, thick, damp, lime-washed walls; the damp stone floor blackened with age; the wobbly domes that looked ready to collapse; the faded curtains and dingy glass of the almirahs through which it was difficult to read the titles of the rows of books inside. All this was enough to make me restive and uneasy, so were the people who came here to read, most of whom were old and tired-looking, their eyes from behind their thick spectacles giving off waves of dejection as they scanned the newspapers. I wanted to escape this tired, old, greying world. Who would want to drown their life in such a dull, lifeless, grimy world? Who would ruin their whole life in this place, I used to ask myself. Each time, I would get the same answer: no one. Or some mad person. Someone like Sudipt, who came from a radiant city like Paris and still didn't feel stifled in this murky library. I often thought about wanting to step into a new, open world, into a shining, changing world, the kind of world promised to us by Pandit Nehru and so many others after him. I would not be able to stay in this old, antiquated world. Sudipt was a little perturbed when he found out, but he never tried to break this dream of mine. Though he would hint at the hollowness of my dreams in jest. But just serious enough that I might become aware of their drawbacks. I found what he said attractive though not necessarily true.

In the very first week of my job, I went to Sudipt three or four times to complain about the good-for-nothing office boys. Sudipt heard me out attentively every time. I felt he just listened to me but never scolded anyone. They still sat around idly, but I found that the dirty almirahs I had complained about were shining. I tried to find out how this had happened. I discovered that Sudipt had come early to the library and cleaned them.

'Why did you do that? The office boys will become even lazier,' I retorted.

Sudipt kept his eyes on the table. Gazing at the table, he said, as if regretting what he had done, 'It was just a little work!'

'But it isn't your work.'

'I had some time.'

'We will never be able to set up a proper process like this.'

'But it won't happen by scolding them either. We educated people haven't educated these office boys enough for them to learn to love books.'

He got up. Went out of the chamber. He walked towards the balcony. The desire to smoke a cigarette must have intensified. I followed him.

'So Alim, don't you think that after Independence, if we had worked as hard in trying to understand our fellow countrymen instead of controlling them, we would have been a different nation?'

I thought for a bit, then said, 'But wasn't it also our responsibility to keep the nation united?'

Sudipt kept the cigarette in his mouth. As if he had forgotten to take the smoke in. He took his hand slowly from the balcony grille to his cigarette and said, 'You can't keep the country united only through force. Alim, don't get upset, but for people like you and me, does our country mean anything more than a map? We want to keep that map as it is under any circumstance. It's not that we don't understand the sorrows of the people here, we do of course, but we don't know their languages.'

'Of course we know. You yourself speak such good Hindi.'

'No, not that, the language of their life.'

He stood quietly for a little longer, gazing out of the balcony. The cigarette continued to burn in his hand. Seeing him so quiet, I went inside. What is the language of life? The more I thought about it, the more confused I became. But without clearing the confusion, I soon put it aside. As I said, I found Sudipt's words attractive but not necessarily true. If I were being honest, I never saw my future in the library while Sudipt was alive. But with his passing, I no longer want to leave this old, dilapidated building, with its almirahs full of rows of books dreaming of being fully realised when they find readers, or the old, greying, unconcerned men bent over their newspapers. Now I don't want to leave this stately old building or the strong lime-washed walls that have supported it for years on end. My dream of going somewhere else vanished in front of my eyes. Old things acquire a new, different meaning in an individual's absence. Is it one of death's miracles that it brings to light the novel meanings hidden inside familiar objects, meanings we were completely unaware of? Could it be that objects have no meanings in themselves – they appear a certain way because they're connected to a particular person, and when they're separated from that person, they appear different. So, is it just about the way you look at things? Are they nothing in themselves? No, how can this be. But with Sudipt's passing, something has changed, either in this world or within me. Could it be that a part of me has left and settled in some other neat, clean world, and the leftover part has become so attached to this old world that it doesn't want to leave and go anywhere else. Has Sudipt cut me into halves and left? Perhaps not. I myself don't want to leave this place. Now I want to stay. I want to spend the rest of my life in this beautiful labyrinth of books. From living abba's dreams, I have shifted to seeing my own. Every morning, I want to get ready in a jiffy and rush here. I am surprised at myself. Like the way I used to be surprised at Sudipt. Always. He could have gone anywhere he wanted. He could have lived however he wanted. I used to be surprised that he didn't leave and go somewhere else. I asked him too..

'Where should I go?'

'Anywhere. Are there no better places than this?'

'There are, but I like it here.'

'This old library where you have to petition those foolish trustees twenty-five times just to procure ten new books?'

He would laugh and reply, 'If they don't ask for clarifications, how will they pass their days?'

'And what of your time?'

'There is a lot of that left, Alim, don't you worry. They will get exhausted trying to get small clarifications from me, and I will be fine giving it to them.'

But he wasn't absolutely fine, was he? And in his passing, was Mridula ji …? No, no, I am being unnecessarily suspicious. It is true she was troubled about Vandana, and she had tried to hint at it when talking to me. But I had deliberately played dumb, because she was placing her suspicions where they had no place. What had she even seen? If only she had come to the library and heard the two of them talking, seen the two of them working. If you saw them working together, you would realise that whoever said writers should be responsible because writing has the power to change the chemistry of one's soul was totally correct. The two were born from literature. They would argue about the excerpt they wanted to include in the Show along with all its possible meanings for hours. They would reassure themselves again and again that it was in tune with the following excerpt. They would gather and review all the excerpts to be read during the Show many times. They would read them out to each other again and again, and only then were the excerpts finally arranged in a sequence.

Even after that Vandana would come running to the library in blazing summer afternoons to express some doubt to Sudipt or point out some weakness that she had noticed. Wisps of hair clinging to the perspiration on her face, which had turned red from the heat. The relatively cool air in the old building would start drying the perspiration and ruffling the now-freed wisps of hair. On such occasions, I would often send them something to drink. Vandana would brighten up and look towards my glass chamber. Sudipt's hand would stay on the table, the cigarette stuck in his fingers pointing at the ceiling, waiting to be lit. If I went and joined them, a delighted Sudipt would slide an open book towards me, saying, 'Alim, look, how beautifully this is written.'

One day, I couldn't stop myself from saying, 'Sir, all this is very well, but why don't I feel it as deeply as the two of you? Why is that so?' Sudipt immediately sat up straight in his chair. He looked grave. Then he said, 'This is true. Only Vandana ji can give you the answer.'

Vandana raised her eyes, first looked at Sudipt, then at me and, disregarding the rules of the library, laughed so openly that the entire building suddenly shook, and Sudipt and I automatically placed our fingers on our lips.

It seemed as if they weren't trying to put together extracts from books but trying to arrange fragments of the immense universe. Seeing the two of them working, I saw, very closely, what it meant to be around so many books, and it is strange how it was in the light that emanated from their reading together that I sensed the grandeur of this library. It was no longer an old, decaying building where I worked; it changed into a place that encompassed the endless curiosity of human beings.

If only Mridula ji had come, just once, on one of those summer afternoons. I often saw her quietly entering the hall on the evenings of Vandana's Show. There, all she would have seen was the result of Sudipt and Vandana's closeness, not the hidden threads of their dedication and pain. Else she wouldn't have met Kishore Lal. He had come to see me and after that, even my abba. His concern was valid. Vandana was his niece; he wanted to keep her in a corner of the world he had built. It is also true that he had constructed this world very diligently. It was understandable that he was extremely flustered by the mere thought of anything causing tremors in this world. But Vandana had already stepped out of the boundary he had woven around himself, never mind how splendid it was. They lived in the same house but in different realms, and their language may have been the same on the surface but, in fact, it wasn't. When I asked her why she never called Kishore to the Show and she answered, 'Alim bhai, there's no point asking him', I realised that as she was sinking deeper into the river of curiosity and familiarity, the distance between their realms was ever growing.

I often sat up with a start whenever I thought whether Kishore's anger and confusion, fanned by Mridula ji's suspicions, had played a role in Sudipt's death. Or did Sudipt have another life I didn't know anything about. Or ... Death may close the doors to a life, but it flings open the doors to all the stories and incidents of that life. Whenever an image of Sudipt's blood-soaked body flashes before my eyes at night, I sit up bolt upright on my bed, and all night I think that how can beauty save the world, when the world is so swift in annihilating it the moment it sees it.

But I won't be able to leave this place where I saw something beautiful flourish, even if it was for a short while. My shoe sticks to the damp floor of the library for a split second before I lift it, and I think that the floor too wants to bind me down and is trying to tell me so in the softest, gentlest manner.

The children are playing on the grass outside, and the sound of a child squealing in delight is suddenly heard in the verandah, carried there by a gust of wind.

Noa

Who can I ask except Lakhna. I can't ask amma anything. As soon as I say something about Baba, she starts crying. Bakul doesn't know anything. Her older sister starts making haste, as if trying to escape somewhere, the moment she sets eyes on me. My schoolteacher calls me before or after every class and gently strokes my back. My girlfriends and other friends stop talking when they see me. Bua comes to take me out in the evenings but often just looks at me, silent and lost. Sometimes, while walking, she catches hold of me and hugs me so tightly to her bosom, my ribs start hurting.

Who can I ask except Lakhna!

Lakhna too listens to everything but says nothing. Many times, he starts sobbing after listening to my questions and then himself starts asking, crying all the while, 'What can I tell you, bibi ji, I'm just a servant. How do I know the truth?' Where could he have gone that so many days have passed, and he hasn't phoned even once – 'Tell me, Lakhna, where could he have gone?' 'Bibi ji, maybe there's no phone there.' 'But there must be paper there. He could have just written a letter. I can read now, can't I?' 'Bibi ji, of course you can read. You have to study a lot, just like saheb. But bibi ji, all places aren't the same, letters can't come from some places.' 'What are you saying, Lakhna, how can there be a place from where letters can't come? Tell me, Lakhna, how can there be such a place? Where can such a place be?' 'How can I tell you? I'm not educated to know all this!'

Does Lakhna know everything, and he is not telling me, just using his illiteracy as an excuse? Or maybe he really doesn't know. Apart from him, there is nobody else who can tell me where Baba has gone, why he has gone, why he went away leaving me asleep, why he didn't meet me before going, when he is coming back. Yesterday, Lakhna was saying, 'Everyone has to go, bibi ji, is there anyone who has escaped this. But why did this happen? This kind of farewell, for such a good man!' 'What kind of farewell, Lakhna, tell me, what kind of farewell?' Lakhna stood silent. Like a statue. Baba used to say, 'Lakhna saheb, how do you suddenly turn to stone? What style – you can be seen walking about whenever you want and turn into a statue whenever you want!' I catch hold of him and shake him hard, pummel his back with my fists, but he remains standing, still and silent, as if he is really made of stone, and nothing I do has any effect on him. Baba used to say, 'Lakhna is a nice man. He takes you out. Why are you always after him. He is ignorant, but he is a good soul.' Lakhna is a good person; he carries me on his back, allows me to sit on his back, as if he were a horse, for hours on end. He carries me in his arms to the maidan, and every time I look at him while playing, I see him sitting at the same place. I don't know why he waves his hand these days when he sees me playing. He doesn't drop me and go away; he stays put on the stairs all through. As though he has no other work. When I asked him, he said, 'Bua ji has told me to stay.' 'Why?' 'How do I know? I'm just a servant, I do what I am told.' 'If no one says anything to you, Lakhna, what will you do then?' 'Bibi ji, my soul will fly away like a bird!' 'What does that mean, Lakhna?' 'How do I know?' 'But you just said it. Show me your soul that flies, Lakhna, or I will complain to Baba. Don't blame me if he scolds you then.' 'Bibi ji, why do you complain to him, saheb gets so worried.' Lakhna stood quietly for a long time. 'How can I show you, I can't show you.' 'Okay, show me your soul that flies tomorrow, or else I will tell Baba ...'

I asked him again the next day when he was taking me to the maidan, and he said, 'First play, I will tell you afterwards.' I ran around all over the maidan. While playing I kept looking at Lakhna from time to time to see if he had run away in fear. But he was there, lying on the stairs. Then I saw him getting up all of a sudden. The ball slipped from my hands. Bakul, standing far away, yelled, 'Noa, where are you looking! Catch the ball!' I looked away from Lakhna and ran after the ball. I played a little more but kept looking at Lakhna every now and then. Eventually, I ran up to him in the middle of the game, and he stood up. 'Bibi, come quickly, I am going to answer your question!' I said happily, 'Show me your soul that flies!' He was quiet for a bit, then said, 'Bibi ji, the thing about the soul that flies is that as long as it's there you can't see it, but when it flies away, you realise that it was there and now it's no longer there.' 'It was there, but now it's no longer there – what does this mean?' I asked him. 'It was there, but it's no longer there,' I asked amma. She didn't say anything. 'It was there, it's no longer there, what does this mean?' I asked bua. 'Who taught you this riddle?' 'Forget that, bua, just tell me!' 'All right, tell me again.' 'It was there, now it isn't.' 'Wait, I'll tell you, wait, okay!' She looked at her feet, then she stood looking out of the window for a while. 'Fruit?' 'No bua, try again.' 'Money?' 'No bua, not at all!' 'Okay, give me a hint!' I said, 'I'll repeat it again. What is that thing that when it's there you can't see it, but once it flies away, you realise that it was there and now it isn't. Tell me, what is it?' Bua gaped at me and said, 'Bhaiya, I give up!' 'Should I tell you?' 'Tell me.' I said instantly, 'The soul that flies.' Bua kept looking at me, as if I had said something nice, something good. I saw her eyes filling with tears. Quickly she wiped her eyes and asked me, 'Who taught you this riddle?'

The formal intimation that the Show is about to begin comes thrice, each time with the sound of fluttering pages. The back door of the hall half opens.

Sneha

Sudipt was the one who told Vandana to do the Show. He is the one who encouraged her to read books. He is the one who awakened everything within her – everything that was so deep, so beautiful – and now he is not there. No wonder Vandana has gone a little crazy. 'This needn't have happened,' she says over and over again. For one, she never speaks, but when she does, this is what she says: It needn't have happened. Maybe she will never be able to come out of this whirlpool of 'it needn't have happened'. But what if she drowns in this whirlpool, and we are unable to do anything. She hasn't even done her Show for the last few months.

I went to her house to meet her. She was sitting in a chair on the terrace, staring at the sky. Seeing me, she smiled but just enough to let me know that she had registered my presence and so that her sorrow could stay hidden behind a thin screen, as if it was something private that she didn't want to show to anyone. In that still afternoon perhaps even the birds were hiding in their nests. The sun had spread its gauzy light from one end of the sky to the other. Occasionally you could see a kite gliding deep in the sky, then it would vanish into some cavern of the sky's shining sprawl. All afternoon I sat there telling her that she should do the Show because it was Sudipt's gift to her. That as soon as she did the Show, she would find some solace. She should think of her audience, which has been coming to the Show for years and is waiting for it even now. Doesn't she owe any responsibility to them? Not even a bit? She smiled as though she felt I was putting forth these arguments to divert her attention. Profound sorrow, in order to keep itself intact, gives human beings a strange insight that is capable of deflecting every effort made to dispel it and rendering every argument against it ineffective.

I kept talking, and Vandana, without saying much, kept looking around. I'd met Biddu at the door. I could see his dense chest hair peeping out of the open buttons on his shirt. At first his eyes rested on my breasts but they soon moved to my open hair flowing over my shoulders. He wanted me to stop and talk to him but I gestured towards the terrace and almost ran away from him, rushing up the stairs. Vandana kept staring at the sky, at the kites gliding there, as if she had forgotten I was sitting in front of her. And as soon as she came back to earth, she would see me and look faintly embarrassed as if she regretted disappearing like this while I was there, but she couldn't help it. Was this the same Vandana, the one who wouldn't stop talking if you brought up the topic of the Show. 'How many days are left for the Show?' '... I've hardly done any preparation.' 'I have to go to the library. Get some books ... I have to select the excerpts.' 'This time I'm doing it on "The Nature of Night".' 'Have you seen the poster? It has a beautiful picture.' 'Sudipt works so hard at all this. He spent all afternoon in the library choosing a picture. I kept telling him it isn't that important, but he wouldn't listen. He said, "The poster should have the right picture!" ...

'For this Show, I am collecting descriptions of nature at night. I have found some beautiful excerpts from Tolstoy's *War and Peace*, Bhasa's *Avimaraka*, Shudrak's *The Little Clay Cart* and Yiannis Ritsos's poetry. I still have to look for many more. Sneha, you come to the Show only sometimes and you leave after a while. But do you know how much work goes into it? It's not easy for a girl like me. It's all because of Sudipt, otherwise I would've never had the courage to do a Show like this. Sneha, sometimes we ourselves don't know what we're capable of. Then someone comes along, opens the closed doors of our soul for us, leaving us astonished at finding what we had never even imagined to be inside us. This can't happen with a tree or an animal. Their ways of being are purely biological. This is what is unique about being human; we ourselves don't know which way will lead us to our potential and which will leave us lost in blind alleys. It's Sudipt's company that has directed me to this path, this task.' … 'We were sitting in the park that day – no, I won't tell you which park, just listen – we were sitting in the park when suddenly Sudipt asked me, "Don't you like to read?" I was quiet, I was thinking. How do I know if I like reading or not. Tell me, Sneha, how many of us have seen the blueprint of our minds that we can immediately answer if someone asks us what we like or don't like. Those who can, they mostly look at other people's likes, imagine their own blueprint and go through their lives adopting others' likes as their own. I can't do it. I stayed quiet. This is what is so special about Sudipt. He is never in a hurry. He asked me this question and kept smoking his cigarette. Seeing that I was silent, he got up and went to the other side of the park to watch the ducks swimming in a small pond. I could see his back and the burning cigarette, held in his hand, go up to his mouth and back. Suddenly I thought of something. I picked up my bag and ran to him. I was about to say something when he spoke, "Look, how beaut—" I hurriedly put my hand over his mouth. You heard me, Sneha, I was in such a hurry, I stopped him mid-sentence. He stared at me in astonishment, and his words retreated, trailing a path inside to reach his eyes where you could see them. My hand still on his mouth, I looked at the words he had been about to say take shape in his eyes. He puffed up his cheeks and blew out the smoke as fast as he could. My hands, which had now loosened their grip on his mouth, trembled and fell. He asked softly, "Yes, so tell me, what were you going to say?" I turned red and blurted out, "I don't know!" Bewildered, he said, "What don't you know?" "I don't know whether I have the desire to read or not!" "This is very good, at least you know that you don't know. Come to the library from tomorrow." "What?" "Bhai, we will have to find out whether you have the desire to read books or not." I went to the library the next day. Sudipt had gone out somewhere. I went and quietly sat at a table. A lot of elderly people were sitting in the library, holding newspapers close to their eyes and reading. I couldn't bring myself to read. I kept looking at Sudipt's chamber and feeling irritated. What a strange man, he called me here and now he has vanished. Where could he have gone? He must remember that he had called me to the library. It was unlike him to do this, had he met with an accident? All kinds of thoughts came and went like waves inside my head. I told myself that I was unnecessarily getting worried. In the middle of all these doubts, I found my hands, I don't know how, were holding a novel. To take my mind off my thoughts, I began reading. The beginning was written in a confused, incoherent language. It was a story about the Kosi River. Someone was narrating the story of centuries-old rivers in a very strange language. I kept reading. Without realising it, I became immersed in the book. I reached a point where Mother Kosi cries out helplessly, "Someone light a lamp, someone," and then another river Dulari Daay arrives holding a lamp, and my eyes welled up. Teardrops fell on the open book in my hands. Hurriedly, I started wiping the pages with my dupatta. When the curtain of tears in front of my eyes dried, I saw Sudipt sitting across the table. He whispered, "Did you find out?"

I had found out.

A space, pulsating, had opened in front of me, which had been shut all these years.'

When I tried to remind Vandana of all this, the thin, brittle smile behind which she had hidden her sorrow went away. Now Vandana was in front of me, sunk in her grief, open, unfiltered. It was as though I was looking at some scarred god. To say she was sad would be a misuse of language: she wasn't just sad, sadness *was* her. As if sorrow had taken on her face and features and appeared in a physical form. Completely. Seeing this, I got a little panicky.

That's when I understood that I had a deep attachment to Vandana's love, her yearning, but I would never be able to feel the same way about anyone else. Deep within me, the flame of that possibility was once burning but then snuffed out.

The afternoon had descended from the terrace and lay stretched out in front of her house, lengthening bit by bit. After a few seconds had passed, I began feeling a little ashamed. Perhaps it wasn't possible to tie her up and bring her over to this side; she had already gone too far into the other side.

The corner seat in the first row was always occupied by the same person. He would sit with his head bowed. The stage was in darkness, the hall was in darkness too, and the spectators let their feet guide them in the darkness to find their seats.

Hall

It is beyond the hall's capability to count the months. What is certain is that many months and the first Saturdays of all those months have passed, and the Show has not been held. Everybody called it that: Show. I was empty and deserted those Saturdays. The girl didn't come nor did her voice, the innermost layer of which quivered with fear and hesitancy. No sound of footsteps. Nor the murmurs of people talking or laughing amidst the tinkling of cups and plates. No whispers filled me from inside, no sudden silence in which the girl's trembling voice would slowly emerge, like a copper moon coming out from behind the clouds.

On the first Saturday of every month, the watchman, instead of sweeping the stage, would lie down in one corner of the stage. In no time, this tired man's snores would fill my interiors. The sound of his snoring, the sound of the words gently spilling out from the girl's bent head, filled my memories. What had happened? Where had everybody gone? This is the problem with being a building. You can't go anywhere to find out what happened. You only know that which you find out by staying here, that's all. The trees nearby rustle in the wind, the birds sitting on their branches give off little shrieks every now and then, squirrels frolic on my walls, but none of them can tell me: What happened? I can sense water flowing, not close by, a little distance away; perhaps a river just happy to be rippling along serenely. It doesn't seem as if it is near me nor does it seem far. For a hall, places that are merely a step away seem far away. Nothing is close. For me, even the road outside is very far. How far a person or place is doesn't depend on metres or kilometres, it depends on your ability. For some, even the moon is close by, and for some, going from me to the nearby toilet can be difficult. A singer was performing on the stage inside me when a man got up and started stumbling to the door. He was moving in the direction of the toilet with great difficulty. But while he was stumbling along, he kept getting distracted by the singer. He took fifteen minutes to cover a distance of twenty metres. What has happened to those people that the distance between them and myself has grown so vast, that they haven't been able to cover it in so many months. So much has happened inside me, all kinds of music have been played, so many different styles of dance performed, so many speeches delivered, the strands of so many different voices float in my inner space. There is a grain of profound joy in all of them. Sometimes there are many such grains. You have to look for them. They get hidden in the general noise, but they are there somewhere, maybe even in the audience's curiosity. That is why I am not affected by rain or burning heat or biting cold. The constant rustling of dry leaves doesn't bother me. But there was something else apart from joy in her Show. What was it? I can't say. There was definitely something different about that Show. Perhaps it had a fragility, as if something very fine was being woven in front of you, which could break at a mere touch, but it stayed intact till the Show got over. As if the spectators were trying to save that delicate weave from the impact of their very breath. It used to take place on Saturday. I used to wait for it almost every afternoon. It's not that I had a distinct liking for it, but this much is true, the words that were uttered in it felt like a balm to me. They didn't hurt me. It always took place on time. First the girl would come running and open my door. Hearing her voice, the watchman would shed his tiredness and begin walking to the stage with his broom. The girl would run to the balcony, go into the box and switch on all the sound equipment, then run down again.

Often I could hear the rustling of her sari or the clacking of her chappals as she went up and down the stairs. Often I would just hear her panting for breath. By this time the stage would have been swept. The watchman would get off the stage and put on all the lights. A torrent of yellow light would fall on her, making her face glow, rays of light sliding off the thin film of perspiration covering it. Meanwhile, the watchman would drag a chair from outside and place it right in the middle of the stage. Often the girl would look at him and smile, often she would laugh and say something to him. He would leave the stage and increase the brightness of the spotlight falling in the middle of the stage. The chair would float in the intense beam of light. The girl would insist he turn down the intensity of the light. The watchman would start dimming the light and keep checking with the girl. At that moment, the front door would often open, and a boyish-looking man would enter, his head bowed a little and quietly sit in the corner seat in the front row. An unlit cigarette dangling between his fingers. He would take out a box of matches from his pocket and put it back in. He would sit like this for a while. He would keep looking at the girl running around and the watchman strolling about. Quietly, he would get up, step outside me and stand smoking his cigarette in the courtyard under the big, leafy tamarind tree. The smoke would dissolve in the air and waft up to me. I would wait for him to come back. Till today I am waiting for him to come back. Why hasn't he come? Where has he gone? What has happened?

People used their eyes to tell others to sit next to them. If someone was sitting alone, trying to read a book, he would have to close it because of the lack of light and then he would look at the dark stage in front of him.

Vandana

You would have to call it a voice. Yes, it was a voice. As soon as it became night, the voice would gently start surrounding me. As if bright strands of cotton from the semal tree had come floating up in the darkness and now clung to me. It was softer than a whisper. A wavy line coming out of the area of silence. At first, I thought I was imagining it. But was there any possibility left for delusions in my present condition? I thought that no, this is not a delusion. Not at all. His passing was like a spear that had deeply pierced my breast; I felt more awake than ever. As if after piercing my breast, it had emerged from my eyes. I was wide awake. How could this be a delusion? No, it wasn't my imagination.

Why just the night? Why did that voice come to me only at night? Like the insect song heard clearly at night, could it be by a shared symmetry of sounds that I could hear the voice too? Who knows? But I don't think that was the case. Maybe among the numerous faint sounds of the night, I had started hearing that 'almost voice' too? Who knows?

It sounded intimate, but I couldn't say who it belonged to. Perhaps it was a kind of intimacy that wasn't connected with anyone, an intimacy that was not tied to anyone. Like what you may find in the sweet water of mountain springs. Like the finely drawn smile on the face of an unknown child or like the shade of trees. A kind of divinity, streaming and scattering from the dust of the lane all the way up to the blue particles of the sky.

I began to wait for the night so that I could hear, rather, experience, that voice. I don't know how, but after a long time, I was waiting for someone. I would think that the faster the day passed, the better. Staring at the sky, I would wish the flocks of birds would carry away the day that stretched to the horizon, so that the night, woven with the fine tendrils of moonlight, could emerge again. Those days when Sneha used to visit me, I wanted to tell her something, but I would stop at the last minute. Suppose I stopped hearing the voice that was softer than a whisper. Suppose that too was snatched from me.

It almost resembled a call. Yes, it was something like that, as if it was calling out to me. Like someone was calling from far away, from beyond the clouds, the mountains, the waterfalls. But by the time it reached me, its words became so faint that it was almost impossible to hear them. I couldn't make out the direction from where the voice was coming, so that I could try and listen in that direction or walk towards it. Even so, I would quietly slip out of the house late at night and, on a hunch, start walking in a particular direction. I would find that the voice wasn't any clearer, and I would walk in the other direction the next night. After I had walked quite far in that direction, I would feel it was coming from somewhere else. Walking in the other direction, I would feel like it was coming from a third direction. Many nights I ran around all over the place in different directions. Its intensity wouldn't wax or wane in any direction. Whichever direction it came from, it was surrounded by different kinds of sounds, as if it came from a different ambience, but though the ambience was different, the voice stayed what it was: an intimate, incomprehensible tremble.

There was a kind of solace in that call – or whatever you want to name it. No, solace is not the right word, there was something else in that call. Something else, in which there was solace but also something more. There was something that cooled my being. I would feel a coolness deep inside me as soon as I heard it. As though the spear stuck inside me was slowly dissolving. Not because I was going far away from his absence, but because listening to that call night after night, or rather, sensing that call night after night, made him seem even closer. As though he was standing next to me, looking at me and smiling.

'What's happening?'

Many times at night I would fall asleep out of sheer exhaustion. This had started happening after some months. Earlier too, my eyelids would droop, but I would float on the surface of sleep like a piece of wood buffeted about here and there by the waves. When I woke up, my eyes would be puffy and swollen, as if they had borne the brunt of being lashed by the waves of sorrow. But now I went deep into slumber, where his absence, spread over every direction, had shrunk into a single cold drop of liquid that kept dripping on my forehead, its chill extending all over my body. I would feel the chill long after I woke up every morning, and for a few moments, I would forget that I had fallen into that pitch-dark deep sleep, leaving my deserted world behind.

Often the sound of someone giggling in the verandah would spill over into the hall. Smiles would appear on a few faces. Perhaps nobody had said this to them, but everyone would tiptoe inside, quietly find their seats and sit down.

Alim

I am going to the Show after two and a half years. Vandana ji is doing it, who else would. I haven't seen her for around two years. That day too, I saw her by chance. Holding Sneha's hand, she was walking on the side of the road. I was also walking down that road, on my way to the hospital to meet my abba. She was looking down. Sneha saw me from afar. She bent and whispered something in Vandana ji's ear. By then I had come a little closer to them. Vandana ji slowly raised her eyes and glanced at me. Her gaze seemed to waver as she looked at me. I folded my hands in greeting, and she smiled with an effort. That was it.

After giving the keys to the watchman, I go down the stairs. I can't say if my mind is awash with sorrow or joy. Perhaps a few ripples of joy are emerging in the river of sorrow. Sudipt's absence is once again going to come out, pure, open, ready to be felt, from within the daily chores and routines where I had hidden it to forget about it. I don't know how I will face it. But I am happy that after so many months, Vandana ji will once again sit in the spotlight. Once again, the pages will flutter in her hands. On the way I met Nawab saheb who was walking to the library. 'Kyon miyan, you have left early today? Have you closed the library?' 'No, saheb, the library is open, please do go and meet the newspapers lying open on the table, waiting for you.' 'And you?' 'I am on my way to see or should I say listen or let me say see and listen to Vandana ji's Show.' 'What's this Show, tell me!' 'I would have told you, but I am in a hurry. If you have the time, you can come with me. You can see for yourself.' 'And my newspapers?' 'I'll keep today's newspapers for you till tomorrow, just come with me now.' Nawab saheb has been a chess player; for him life was all about unfamiliar moves. I had seen him in all sorts of places, always full of enthusiasm. He was interested in horse racing, and you would also see him at Ustad Zia Mohiuddin's veena concert. He was fond of cricket, and he would also listen attentively to serious lectures organised by the university. I had never taken the trouble to find where his estate was, but he had such an elegant way of doing things, you would have called him a Nawab even if you didn't know he was one.

She had come to the library yesterday. She was carrying a heavy cloth bag and sweat was trickling down her face, which had turned red as if it had soaked in a bit of the sun. She seemed to have walked very fast. She entered my cabin and said, 'Alim, you have to come tomorrow evening.'

'At least sit down first.'

'I don't have time for that. You have to come tomorrow!'

'I'll come but where?'

'Where I used to do my Show!'

After Sudipt sir's going, I had changed the librarian's chamber a bit, so that the chair he used to sit on would stay empty, and you wouldn't be able to spot it easily either. While talking to me, Vandana turned her gaze to the empty chair, looked down at the legs of the chair, paused for a bit, then looked at me and said, 'I'm going to start the Show again.'

She was talking to me as if she was in fact giving this information to someone else. And she turned and left the library. I kept calling out to her, but saying, 'Another time, another time,' she got into an auto-rickshaw parked by the road and went away. I felt she had run away in order to control herself. Sudipt sir's empty chair had probably created a storm in her or perhaps unleashed a flood of sorrow. But a slight glow had returned to her face, like the early morning sun shining from behind dense clouds.

'I'm coming with you, miyan, at least tell me where we're going.'

Nawab saheb's patience was wearing thin. But I wasn't looking at him. I was walking, lost in myself. We came to the hall. A small hall where a good film would often be screened on Sunday evenings, but which always lay empty on Saturdays. That is why sir had fixed Vandana ji's Show for this day. There were a few cars, scooters and bicycles parked in the small courtyard. Some people had gone in, some were still strolling about outside. I heard Nawab saheb's voice again.

'Miyan, if you're not in a hurry, let's have a cup of tea first!'

I had forgotten that visitors were always served tea outside the hall before the Show started. I myself used to stand behind the table and serve tea. It made me feel like I too was helping in some way. I looked at the tea table and saw Sneha. Taking Nawab saheb with me, I went up to her. When Sneha handed us a cup of tea, I told her, 'You have been unfair to me.'

Sneha handed a cup to Nawab saheb and said, 'Have you come to see the Show or to level accusations against me. Okay, tell me, what have I done?'

I immediately retorted, 'You have taken on the work I used to do, and I have been rendered useless.'

Sneha laughed and said, 'Don't worry, you will get your work back in the next Show!'

'Good that you agree, otherwise I was contemplating a lawsuit. Won't I get a cup of tea, or will I have to make do with mere talk?'

'You'll find out later if this tea has taste or if it's poison!' By saying this, she disarmed me completely.

Sneha had just handed me a cup when we heard the second bell ring. She took the cup back and said laughingly, 'It seems you're not fated to have tea today!'

I hurried to the door of the hall. Nawab saheb too abandoned his tea midway and followed me inside. He had been watching everything quietly. He had stopped asking me anything. Perhaps this is what you call elegance: to wait patiently for some unknown event to unfold. The lights are still on inside. We sit down in the third row. Two rows ahead, Mridula ji is sitting with Noa in her lap. Quite a few people are standing around her, conversing in low voices. Noa is turning her head this way and that. Mridula ji keeps looking ahead. Her face is bright, and the radiance in the empty parting of her hair looks like it's falling on Noa's face.

The darkened stage quivers in front of my wet eyes.

There's one woman who always enters carrying heavy bags on her shoulders. A tired-looking man walks in behind her. First, she places her bags on the seat next to her, then she sits down herself. The tired-looking man stands nearby, looking at her.

Sushila

It was I who said, 'Vandana *will* go.' I was quite amazed at my own sharp tone. He, Biddu and Kish were all there, and once again, they were making a plan to stop Vandana.

Biddu was saying, 'Let her go out just once and you wait and see, there'll be some new headache.'

Kish is clever. He keeps quiet and lets Biddu say the petty things that he wants to say. After Biddu is done saying what he has to, he steps into the conversation quietly, like some sensible, intelligent person. Though he wants to do exactly what Biddu has blurted out in his foolishness.

Kish said softly, 'What is the point of starting the Show again?'

Vando's father gave it some thought for a moment. Perhaps he was slightly comforted by the fact that even if it was due to the Show, Vandana would at least go out of the house, or rather, at least step out of her room. But Biddu and Kish's views were preventing him from taking the right decision. He started vacillating. I was standing in the kitchen, seasoning some vegetables. I realised that he needed me to stand firm. I turned off the gas, came out hurriedly and said, 'Vando *will* go!'

He stared at me. Biddu looked at me with his burning gaze. Kish kept sitting with his head bowed.

'She is trying to get back on her feet, and you people are trying to stop her. I won't let this happen.'

Biddu was about to speak but without looking at him I said, 'Keep quiet, Biddu. You understand nothing and talk too much.'

Vando's father shifted on the sofa and said in a low voice, 'Won't it look bad?'

I had an inkling that such questions would come up. I was prepared for them. I said immediately, 'Why should it look bad? Vandana is doing a Show where she will read out excerpts written by the world's best-known writers, poets and thinkers to people. Will it enhance our reputation or sully it?'

He didn't expect me to make such arguments. Nobody said anything. Kish kept looking down, and Vandana's father gazed at a bird sitting on the window. The bird sat for a while, cocking its head this way and that, then it suddenly seemed to think of something and flew away with its wings flapping.

Biddu is an idiot, for even now he spoke, 'Ma, you don't understand.'

I looked at Biddu lovingly and said, 'I understand. Vando will go wherever she wants.'

Saying this, I turned on my heel, went back to the kitchen and lit the gas stove again with the lighter. The vegetables had turned cold in the pan. I understood that this is what Vandana is going to do all her life. This is the only way she will feel close to Sudipt. I was amazed at how a relationship could transform a simple girl like Vando so much that her very presence had begun exuding a radiance. We may want to believe it or not, but it is true that Sudipt had opened a door inside Vandana, behind which flowed a river of light. This was the river in which Vando's face, hands and feet were drenched.

Taking the thali of food, I tiptoed into Vando's room. She was sitting surrounded by books. I made some space in the middle of the books and put the thali down. Like every day, she looked at me, gave a half-smile and went back to her work. I stood for a while, looking at her. Her hair fell about her face. Only her eyes could be seen but some strands of hair would keep falling over them too, and she constantly pushed them back with her hands. I wanted to go and plait her hair, but I knew that she had gone too far away from us; she was separate from us now, and we would have to put in hard work to connect with her again.

Seeing me standing there, she lifted her head after a while and, looking at me, said, 'Yes, Ma!'

I panicked a little. I didn't realise I had been standing there.

'Vando, can I come to your Show?'

Vandana put the book she was holding on the floor. She took the pen that was held in her mouth, put it between the pages of the book and, turning towards me, said, 'You can come with me!'

'No, Vando, how can I ...?' I said haltingly.

'I'll go quietly; will anyone stop me?'

She kept looking at me. It seemed like she wanted to say a lot, but settled with saying softly, 'You know where the hall is, don't you?'

'Yes, I know. You do your work. I'll come. On my own.'

I stood outside, waiting for everyone to go in. As soon as the third bell rang in the hall, all the people loitering in the courtyard started filing in slowly. Sneha, standing behind the tea table, wiped her hands and began to move away. The watchman stood outside one of the two or three doors that led into the hall. I went up to him and asked softly, 'Bhaiyya, which is the door to the seats at the back?'

He heard me and absent-mindedly opened a door. I sat in a dark corner in the last row. All sorts of people were sitting in the twenty-five or thirty rows in front of me. When a new person entered, people would quietly make space for him to pass. Vando couldn't be seen anywhere. Did someone stop her again? A faint shadow of doubt began growing in my mind. Trying to put it behind me, I looked ahead. I could see a white chair shrouded in darkness on the stage. A few moments passed, and darkness descended in the hall. A spotlight fell on the white chair on the stage, and a voice started speaking from behind the stage. It was Sneha's voice. She spoke about Vandana for a while. I couldn't really follow what she was saying. She paused for a couple of seconds, then said, 'Vandana ji will do today's Show and all Shows to follow in Sudipt's memory. We request you to please stand up for two minutes and remember him. We do this because maybe in the silence you might hear his open laughter.' Everyone got up quietly. I too adjusted my pallu on my head and stood up in front of my seat. The silence there was so intense that I closed my eyes in fear. I saw myself running down the road in a frock. I am actually trying to catch the shadow of a kite falling on the uneven ground of the maidan. It keeps moving, and I keep running. My foot hits a stone and I am about to fall. Somebody catches my hand and holds me and says, 'Ma ji, careful!' And he starts laughing loudly. I hold that laughter and open my eyes: Oh! It was him. Exactly like him.

Vandana came and sat on the chair bathed in a circle of light.

The sound of traffic outside seeps in from the open door at the back. Car horns, the noise of old truck engines, the rough sound of cycle bells ringing. The door shuts and all the outside noises cease.

Lakhna

Lakhna has forgotten how to count the days. You count the days when there is hope, but the house was blanketed in so much grief, you couldn't see any way out of it. Memsaab's face remains unchanged despite Noa bibi's questions, bua's support and courage, and my foolish attempts at explanations. She seems to have turned to stone. She never goes out nor does she take walks in the garden. Nor is she happy seeing the flowers. When saheb was there, memsaab had bludgeoned me into becoming a gardener. 'Lakhna, bring that plant here, plant that creeper there. Lakhna, why didn't you get organic manure? Lakhna, how many days since you watered the jasmine plant?' How could I have so much knowledge about plants as to match memsaab's interest in gardening? She would often ask me, 'You have a farm back home, how come you know so little about plants and trees?'

How can Lakhna tell her that we didn't do any farming, that we were labourers who worked on farms, and I was thrown into it when I was a child, and when I grew up a little, I left my home and country. How much could Lakhna learn in such a situation? But I used to keep at it and work hard so that memsaab was happy. Even after saheb passed away, I kept planting all sorts of plants, which bloomed with colourful flowers, but memsaab never noticed them. I could feel the flowers were desperate for her attention, but memsaab never even looked at them. She was lost in herself. She would get Noa ready for school without saying a word, then wordlessly place her hand in mine, indicating that I should go and drop her to the school bus. After Noa returned, she would change her clothes quietly and just as silently feed her with her own hands. Noa bibi would keep chattering all the while, to which she would merely murmur, 'Yes, yes.' Noa bibi knows that memsaab is lost in some other thoughts. Children can immediately make out when you are not paying attention to them. And then we are talking about Noa bibi – her intelligence has enhanced even more after saheb's passing. In spite of memsaab's lack of attention, Noa bibi doesn't say anything to her. She has more or less stopped throwing any tantrums or being stubborn that things be done her way. Otherwise, she used to drive saheb mad. 'Take me to bua's place' ... 'I want to go to the park!' ... 'I want to stand on a mountain and see the lights at night.'

Saheb would listen and give in to everything she asked for. Sometimes he would take her to bookshops, sometimes carry her on his shoulders and climb to the top of a mountain. If memsaab tried to reason with Noa bibi, saheb would say, 'Noa won't listen to you, of course she will go to her bua's house.' Where has Noa bibi's wilfulness gone? Has saheb's death hit her so deeply that her obstinacy has dried up? People may believe that death doesn't affect children that much, but Lakhna feels children soak up death so deep inside them, they keep feeling it like hot vapours.

I was working in the garden when I heard memsaab sobbing in the verandah. I looked up from the flowerbeds. She was crying in somebody's arms. Still squatting, I inched a little closer. Memsaab was crying on Vandana ji's shoulders. I looked at them for a while, then saw Noa bibi running towards them from the corner of the garden. I yelled, 'Noa bibi, where were you?'

Hearing my voice, memsaab pulled back from Vandana ji. They quickly wiped their eyes.

As soon as Noa bibi reached them, Vandana ji took her in her arms. Memsaab took both of them inside. I went to the kitchen from the back entrance and carried some tea into the living room. Memsaab was sitting, holding Vandana ji's hand. Noa bibi was jumping from a chair on to the floor and then climbing up on the chair again. 'Mamma, I am jumping into a pond,' she would say and jump down. 'Now you are tired from swimming in the pond, drink your milk.' Vandana ji picked up the glass of milk from the tray. A smile lit up memsaab's face. I saw a smile in the house for the first time in two years. I went back to the garden. When Vandana ji came out some half an hour or forty-five minutes later, Noa bibi was in her arms. Memsaab went to the gate to see her off. Noa bibi withdrew herself from Vandana ji and stood there, clinging to memsaab's legs.

'We'll definitely come!' she was saying to Vandana ji.

There was darkness all around. Only the overlapping, soft rustling of people breathing.

Sneha

At first, I didn't believe it. I kept looking at her without saying anything, as if she was uttering words with no meanings. As though they were mere sounds. I saw the last two or three years pass by in a flash inside me: her sitting on the terrace for hours, staring at the sky; walking on the streets without looking left or right; sitting without saying a word for an hour even though I would be there next to her; untangling her hair and giving up halfway, plaiting it any which way; putting a bindi on her forehead without looking in a mirror so that it wasn't in the proper place; sitting for a long time holding an upside-down book in her hands. I had given up hope. I thought perhaps we would have to take her to a psychiatrist for treatment or admit her to some far-off asylum. For months there were no signs of her getting better. I would go to her house, sit with her for a while, then get up and leave. She would be neither happy nor restless at my going. It was like the whole world was hiding behind a wall, and she sat resting her head on that wall day after day. I too stopped going over to see her that often. I had thought she might try to find a way to come out of her loneliness. If she had managed to stay alive for so many days after Sudipt's passing, surely there was some desire, some attachment to life still throbbing within her.

I went to see her after many months. I ran up the stairs to escape from her uncles' knives. She wasn't on the terrace. I went to her room. She was sitting surrounded by books. The morning sun, filtering in from the window, was sliding off her hair. There was a pen between her teeth, three or four books were open in her lap, and the sadness on her face had receded a little. It had been replaced by eagerness. She took no notice of my entering the room. Her eyes stayed fixed on her book. After a little while, she copied some lines from the book onto a piece of paper and then put the pen back between her teeth. I touched her shoulder. She turned to me with a start, then smiled. The pen fell from her mouth onto her lap. I cupped her cheeks in my hands.

'I am doing the Show!' she said forcefully. Then, realising she had spoken a little too loudly, she repeated more softly, 'I am doing the Show.'

I couldn't believe my ears, and instead of saying something, I just stared at her.

'I was hoping you would come. The hall has to be booked for the same day. You remember, don't you? The first Saturday of the month. We will have to inform them that from now on the Show will be held every month on the same day. I hope they haven't given the day away to somebody else. We will have to inform people. Sudipt used to get it advertised in the newspaper too, but I don't know if we will be able to do that. You will manage, won't you! Or I can come with you. But how will I come; I have to select excerpts from many books. This time I am trying to do something special ...'

She was speaking without pause, as if she wanted to say what she had to and be done with it. Or maybe she was speaking so fast because she didn't want any grief to slip in again in the pauses between her sentences. I could only stare at her. It was as if a statue had started speaking in front of me.

'Won't you ask me what will be special this time?'

I stopped to think. I was only listening to Vandana's voice, not the words she was saying.

'Tell me, what is special?' I turned her words into a counter-question.

'This time I am going to include some of the things Sudipt had said.'

Saying this, a thin layer of happiness spread all over her face. Was this a new way for her to get close to him?

She said again, 'Sneha! Now go. You have a lot of work to do. Do everything I have told you to do. I will also get down to finishing all the work that's left for the Show.'

She took the pen that had fallen in her lap, stuck it between her teeth again, opened some books lying on the side and began reading. I got up quietly and, trying to remember all the things I had been told to do, went out. I heard her voice call out from behind me:

'Don't forget to organise the tea.'

I turned to look at her and smiled. Her head was bowed. She had gone back to her pages. The sun shone on her hair.

The watchman comes down the stairs to where the gardener is taking care of the children and holds out his hand. The gardener puts a packet of beedis and a matchbox into his empty hand.

Mridula

When she came in and shut the gate, I saw her back. For a moment I couldn't believe it was her. But when she turned, it *was* her. I wanted to turn around and disappear inside the house. But I stayed where I was, thinking she must have seen me standing in the verandah. Head bowed, she was walking towards the verandah. There was a hesitancy in her walk, as though she was somehow pushing herself forward. Or perhaps the weight of Sudipt's absence was making it difficult for her to move. Or perhaps she couldn't decide if she should meet me or not. I felt I should help her. She would be able to move forward, and I too would feel lighter. The sunlight had reached the stairs and stayed there. Leaves from the neem tree were scattered everywhere. A faint yellowness had spread on the ground. A bird was chirruping in fits and starts. I had just placed my foot on the stairs when Vandana looked up. Now I couldn't stop myself. I ran to her and, without looking into her eyes, caught hold of her hand, brought her to the verandah and hugged her. Before the sound of our sobbing could become louder, Noa came running from the other side. We wiped our cheeks. Vandana picked Noa up. Noa also put her arms around her. Before they could start talking, I rushed inside to the kitchen. I quickly made some tea, opened a whole lot of tins, took out some special biscuits, arranged them on plates and put everything on a tray. I was about to take the tray outside when Lakhna appeared from the back door. He looked at me with genuine sweetness. I glanced at him, then at the tray and went out.

'Will you come?' Vandana was asking Noa.

'Yes, I will come,' Noa answered. Her voice came floating in the air and struck my eardrums.

Lakhna came in quietly and put the tray on the table. I gestured to Vandana to sit down and said, 'Where are you planning to go?'

Noa looked at me and said, 'Amma, I'm going to the Show. Can I go with Vandana didi? Tell me, can I go?'

The Show! The same place where I used to slink in to keep an eye on Vandana and Sudipt, leaving before the Show was over. The Show, which I always wished would shut down, but which was the only way for me to grope for the threads that tied Sudipt and Vandana together. The Show, which gave him so much contentment. So what if Noa goes? Why should I stop her?

'You can go, Noa!'

Vandana put her arms around Noa and held her close. Her face was resting on Noa's open hair. Her eyes were closed. I turned my gaze outside and heard Vandana's voice.

'Mridula ji, will you be able to take out the time? I would feel very happy if you came!'

Her face was still resting on Noa's hair. Her eyes were open. She was looking at me but not into my eyes, her gaze fixed somewhere near my eyes. How could I go? Earlier I used to hide from everyone and sit in the back row, but now?

No, I won't go. But why shouldn't I go? Why should I hide? Wasn't I filled with joy if Sudipt just looked at me? Did my attachment to him have no value in my own eyes? Did it lessen at all with his going? I have to start a new life, establish a new relationship with Sudipt. That can only happen if I try to make the world he created a little more beautiful or at least try and walk through it. Yes, it is only through the Show that I will find my way to this new Sudipt. The Show is the ladder by which I can reach him or at least his shadow. I will definitely go. They can call it shamelessness or whatever else they want to. I have to find a way – no, I have to make my own way to reach him.

'When is it?' I heard myself saying.

Vandana's eyes came to rest on mine. Her eyes were welling up, so were mine. I composed myself with some difficulty. She looked down and said, 'Saturday evening. Seven p.m. It is winter so it will be a little dark by then.'

She suddenly fell silent. Still carrying Noa, she got up and began walking out. By the time she came back after strolling in the verandah, a thin brown film had formed over her tea.

'The tea has become cold,' I said.

She put Noa down and picked up her teacup. She handed Noa a few papers and said, 'Read them aloud three or four times! Okay?'

Eyes dancing, Noa said, 'Okay!'

Lakhna dropped us till the hall. He had carried Noa all the way. Noa had handed her papers to me and was hanging on to Lakhna's neck. Before reaching the courtyard outside the hall, she got down. Lakhna turned to go back. I gestured to him to go and sit inside the hall. Hesitantly, he went in and sat in a dark corner seat at the back. I gave the pages back to Noa. Slowly I started walking in. I was finding it difficult to lift my feet. There was a table outside and a crowd of people around it. Wearing an apron, Sneha was handing out cups of tea. Seeing me, she came out from behind the table and, taking me by the hand, took me there and handed me a cup of tea. I saw many of Sudipt's friends. I sat down on a nearby chair. A few of Sudipt's friends came up to me, greeted me and began chatting. I couldn't hear anything. But I politely went on nodding. The first bell went off, Sneha ran up to me and said, 'Mridula ji, please go in now.'

I looked all around me, I couldn't see Noa anywhere. I went into the courtyard, I saw Noa talking to another girl. We went inside. I walked ahead slowly, intending to sit in the third or fourth row, but a girl who was around Noa's age grabbed my hand and made me sit in the first row. Noa climbed onto my lap right away. Her red ribbon tickled my nose.

A pool of light suddenly falls on the stage. In the yellow circle of light, the papers in the girl's hands start shaking. Slowly, softly, her voice rises as if the air in her throat is being delicately chiselled …

Noa

I was sitting in amma's lap. I kept turning around to see where Lakhna was sitting. Amma said softly in my ear, 'Noa! He is sitting at the back, you won't be able to see him from here … Okay, look right at the back, look carefully. See something? That's Lakhna.'

'You made him sit properly, didn't you?' I asked. Amma was lost somewhere. She didn't hear my question.

In front, the stage was in darkness. Somebody from behind the stage was talking about Vandana didi. She also took baba's name. Suddenly, everyone stood up. I closed my eyes. Ma picked me up in her arms. I opened my eyes a little. She put me in Vandana didi's arms. Didi is taking me to the stage. I close my eyes again.

Baba is walking towards me. He whispers in my ear, 'Noa, don't be afraid … say each word slowly so that you can taste it on your tongue.'

'Baba, taste?'

'Yes, beta, taste!'

I had been made to sit in the chair next to Vandana didi's. Some papers fluttered in my hands. Vandana didi smiled and looked at me. Baba gently stroked my shoulders.

The girl sitting in the circle of light barely opens her lips and a low-pitched voice emerges, collides with the mike and flutters like a butterfly in the ears of the listeners. That evening it was as if a butterfly was fluttering about in little spurts: 'Today, in the end, I am going to recount some of the things the person who first imagined this Show had said … Love is the name for a participation in eternity. That is why death can't tie it down. It becomes a part of it …'

Lakhna

It was saheb himself. It *was* him. You couldn't see him. Not at all. But he was there. It was saheb, it was him. Noa bibi would look at the papers now and then and read out something. It seemed like a very familiar voice was speaking when she spoke. Absolutely familiar. Whose voice was it? Whose? Saheb! Arre! This is his voice. Not only when Noa bibi was speaking, you could hear saheb in Vandana ji's voice too. What is this play of yours, God? Saheb is alive even after his death. Everyone can hear him, everyone can sense him. Lakhna knows that a man goes away in many different ways; he goes to the afterworld. But I am seeing this for the first time: there is a way to make the dead come alive.

Lakhna wants to run to memsaab. He wants to tell memsaab that look, memsaab, saheb isn't gone. Lakhna has heard him today in Noa bibi's bright, flowering voice and in Vandana ji's trembling tones. He was the one speaking, listening, moving his head. Memsaab, what is this miracle!

How can Lakhna go. If saheb sees Lakhna get up in the middle and leave, who knows what might happen. He might not scold Lakhna, but just the sight of those knotted brows on such a good man's face is enough to pierce Lakhna's heart.

No, no, Lakhna couldn't understand anything, but there is power in the spoken word. And then, this is saheb speaking, this is his language; it is filled to the brim with love, indulgence and fondness. Yes, love, fondness. All Lakhna could hear every now and then, the only thing he could hear was:

'Lakhna, why do you call yourself Lakhna!'

'Lakhna, why do you call yourself . . .!'

Translator's Acknowledgements

Many thanks to:

Udayan Vajpeyi, for writing such a beautiful novel. It was a joy to translate, and working with him was a real pleasure. Our discussions and conversations over many dinners – all so enjoyable (and educative)!

Sivapriya, my wonderful editor. I was fortunate to have worked with her on my first translation, and I was delighted to be back with her for *Qayas*. She has a fine eye and goes through the whole process of bringing a book together – from idea to publication – with unruffled calm and expertise. (And yes, there were many lovely dinners involved here too!)

Chakrika, for her extremely meticulous, thoughtful edits.

Arun, for being with me all through, bucking me up whenever I felt overwhelmed and, best of all, cooking the most fabulous meals to keep me happy and content! And dearest Arjun and

Translator's Acknowledgements

Chrissy – though you are in faraway New York, I felt buoyed by your quiet support and encouragement from thousands of miles away.

My parents, always excited when a new book of mine was coming out, are no longer here. But I felt their presence every day that I was writing. And I knew I had their blessings every step of the way. I can never thank them enough for instilling in me a love for reading and writing, surely the greatest joys in the world.